The Nature of Wayfinding

Carolyn Purcell Jaco

Sissortail Press

The Nature of Wayfinding

© 2023 Carolyn Purcell Jaco

ISBN: 979-8-9878743-1-8

First Edition

Published in the United States

Scissortail Press

876 Hartshorne Lake Road

Hartshorne, Oklahoma 74547

541-993-8498

calyjaco@gmail.com

Dedicated to
William E. Purcell
1926 – 2016

Contents

St. Louis

BERTHA HAD TWO OLDER brothers, and five younger siblings that she helped her mother look after. In 1885, at fifteen years old, her long auburn hair hung down her back in a thick braid, twisted up high on her head when she went to the village brewery each day to fetch a pail of lager for the evening meal. Once the children were old enough to work, they drank beer along with their parents. She was well liked, and one of the boys at the brewery hoped to one day marry her.

Her father was a well-known woodworker who filled orders for furniture and cabinets from towns and cities far away. Their village was near the mountains where they harvested materials from the forest. His children learned to plane boards, sand fine finishes, and cut dove-tailed joints starting at the age of twelve. They took the finished products by wagon down to the railroad station five miles away for shipping to customers.

Hamish was a year older than Bertha. He had brown hair and eyes and a round friendly face. He matched her height exactly when they looked into each other's eyes, for she was somewhat tall for a girl. When he saw her approaching, he would quickly remove his cap and nervously run his fingers through his hair. He could not suppress his grin when they met and she was equally smitten. It seemed the most natural thing in the world that one day they would marry and have a family there in the village. Hamish would often ask Bertha to meet him late in the day and they would walk through the forest together and talk.

Friedrich knew of this courtship, but Bertha's father wanted something more for his daughter. She was quick to learn and eager to help her father teach the younger ones. He saw a brightness in her that he did not see in the others. As his first daughter, he had made a special bond with her when she was born that superseded his own desire to keep her close by.

He wanted her to see beyond their life in the village. He schooled her in geography and the politics of other places to help her understand the vastness of the world and the possibilities it held.

Friedrich wrote a letter to his cousin in Hamburg who he knew had ties with German immigrants in America. After six months passed, a reply came that the Busch family in St. Louis, Missouri would welcome Bertha as a nanny for their children. Friedrich sat with Bertha late into the night talking about this opportunity.

"What about Hamish? Father, you know he intends to ask you for my hand in marriage," Bertha said.

"Yes, it would appear so. But do you truly wish to spend your entire life here as the wife of the brewer?" her father asked.

Bertha was torn. She did in fact want to go to America. But the thought of breaking Hamish's heart gave her a pain in her chest. She spent the next week searching her thoughts and feelings. As for Bertha's mother, she was terribly worried. She did not know anyone with the courage to leave everything behind for the unknown. She and her parents, and their parents before that, considered moving to the next village a necessary part of finding a suitable marriage. But nothing beyond that had ever made sense. What if Hamish really was Bertha's destined true love? They seemed to be a good match, but the decision was Bertha's, and Friedrich clearly was swaying her. Finally, in a moment of bravery Bertha told her father she wanted to go. He advised her to avoid saying goodbye to Hamish.

"It could weaken your resolve, my dear. You are doing the right thing," he told her in private.

Bertha continued her friendly manner with Hamish. Friedrich advised they keep it a secret, even from the other children, until it was time to say goodbye. Friedrich would tell Hamish after Bertha was well on her way. He drove her to the train station five miles away and bought her passage to Hamburg. He gave her money for the remainder of her trip and advised her to use it frugally. In Hamburg, she asked directions to the shipyard and found the ticketing office there. It would be two days before the ship sailed, so she was directed to a lady's boarding house nearby. There, she shared a room with a woman who worked as a laundry maid in one of the large hotels. The maid was pleasant enough, but uneducated and rough. She had the skittish demeanor of a beaten dog.

The steamer was bigger than anything Bertha had imagined. It was a thrill to see the view from the deck. The captain intercepted her as soon as she boarded. As a young girl traveling alone, the captain took her under his care to keep her safe. Despite her third-class ticket, he found an available second-class berth with a woman in her twenties named Ulla who was also traveling alone. Ulla was going to join her husband who had immigrated to New York and found work as a clerk at the shipyard. He had sent her the money he saved for her passage. Bertha and Ulla were agreeable traveling companions and enjoyed sharing books and stories with each other to pass the time.

When they arrived in New York, Ulla and her husband took her to the train station.

"Good luck, my friend," Ulla said. "You have a new life in America awaiting you."

They gave each other a long warm hug and Bertha boarded the train for the final leg of her journey.

She arrived in St. Louis travel weary, but also excited to see the bustling city. A coachman greeted her and delivered her to the regal home of Adolphus and Lilly Busch. They had been expecting her and had asked the ticket master to let them know what train she would be arriving on. She was greeted in German and showed to her room where she was brought dinner and allowed to sleep until the next morning.

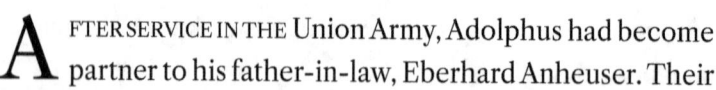

AFTER SERVICE IN THE Union Army, Adolphus had become partner to his father-in-law, Eberhard Anheuser. Their successful high-volume brewing company and far-reaching distribution pattern afforded the partners grand homes and a life in high society. They welcomed immigrants from their homeland and advertised there regarding jobs at the brewing facility in St. Louis.

The Busch family embraced Bertha as one of their own kin. She would run the nursery and provide home education for their large brood of five children and growing. They paid her with a spacious room of her own overlooking the back garden, board from the professionally run kitchen, and stock in the company. They provided her with a fine wardrobe befitting the Busch prestige, and people in the community treated her with respect. Bertha was very happy with her lot in life. She grew close with all the children and lived vicariously through them as the older girls were courted and married. But when Bertha turned twenty-four, Lilly Busch became concerned that they were preventing her from having a family of her own. This led to Adolphus and Lilly doing some matchmaking.

"Bertha, dear, you know you are one of our family and we all adore you. I have watched how much love and care you have for our children and we could never have asked for a better nanny."

"Thank you, Lilly," Bertha replied. For Lilly made Bertha stop calling her Mrs. Busch and Ma'am after only a few months past her arrival. She continued to address her employer formally in the presence of others, but used her first name in private.

"I have recently thought how selfish it would be to deny you the opportunity to have children of your own," Lilly continued.

"Oh, it is not a problem for me. I have so much to do here and do not need to have children," Bertha assured her.

"I think you say that because you never thought it possible, especially as you grew older. You cannot imagine the feeling of having your very own children in your image, not to mention the love of a man. Adolphus and I would like to help find you a husband before it is too late for you," Lilly said gently.

"Thank you for your kindness, but my duty is here. What would you do with the younger children?" Bertha worried.

"Do not give it a thought. We will find another suitable nanny," Lilly said smiling.

Bertha suddenly felt quite overwhelmed and tears filled her eyes. "This is my home."

"Oh goodness, no tears! You will always be welcome here and if you wish, you can come back again later when your children are grown. I promise you," Lilly assured her.

Lilly's desire to help Bertha was strong and felt like the right thing to do. She enlisted her husband's help since he knew all the men at the brewery.

❦❲

HEINRICH MELZL HAD RESPONDED to a placard for brewery work and come by steamer from Germany and up the St. Louis River in 1888 at the age of thirty-four. Now forty years old, he had never been married. Adolphus told his wife that almost all the men at work were married or betrothed. Despite Heinrich's age, Adolphus thought Heinrich might be a good prospect for Bertha. He was honest, hardworking, and because he did not fraternize after work with the other men often, Adolphus thought he might be a bit lonely. Lilly Busch herself invited Heinrich to afternoon tea. Bertha sat up straight perched on the edge of the sofa, while Heinrich sat back, legs crossed and talked of his life. Heinrich was neither handsome nor displeasing to look at. He had medium brown hair and a duster mustache. He was five foot six inches to Bertha's five foot nine. They conversed in German.

"I was born the third boy in a family of ten children. My father milled flour for our village. When I was twelve, my father arranged for me to apprentice at the brewery in the next village, about eight kilometers away.

At seventeen, when the apprenticeship ended, my master chose to find a new apprentice leaving me without work or a home.

I would not return to my parents who had too many mouths to feed, so I went to Dresden to work. I spent ten years there working in the brewing trade. My pay was low, so I moved around trying to improve my circumstances.

"Then I was drafted into our Franco-Prussian War and fought for two years. When the war ended, I went back to the breweries, but did not find steady work. The economy was not good in the German Empire. I was in the public square drinking tea when I saw a placard about jobs in the United States at Anheuser in St. Louis. I wrote and they replied sending some money to help pay for my passage. It was a long trip to Bremen, then up the river and out to sea to New York, and then to New Orleans and twelve hundred miles up the Mississippi River. I was traveling for months with little money.

"When I arrived in St. Louis, I was greeted with such kindness. The family provided me with housing in the apartments they built for workers near the brewery. They put me to work right away with good wages. I have worked here ever since with allegiance to the Busch and Anheuser families."

Bertha told him of her recruitment as a nanny and her shared loyalty to their generous benefactors. Lilly invited Heinrich back four times over the next two months for chaperoned afternoon tea. They made polite conversation about news from Germany and happenings at the brewery.

Adolphus encouraged Heinrich to ask for Bertha's hand. They hardly knew each other, but neither did they have time to be particular. Bertha was becoming an spinster and Heinrich was getting old. Neither would dream of showing any lack of gratitude for the efforts being made on their behalf.

A protestant minister joined them in marriage at the nearby church attended by the immediate Busch family, and a few of Heinrich's friends from the brewery. They stood there together before the minister in 1894, Bertha in a borrowed white dress standing three inches taller than Heinrich in his black suit, and touched each other for the first time when he chastely kissed her hand at the completion of the ceremony.

Bertha moved to the three-bedroom clapboard house Heinrich found for them in a quiet neighborhood on the edge of the city. Heinrich was a stern man and held strong traditional values about marriage and family. Bertha worked hard to recall her long unused cooking skills learned from her mother at a young age. They planted a garden each spring of potatoes, cabbage, and herbs, and kept six laying hens. She gave Heinrich three children, all girls, which he named Halley, Olga, and Elsie, born in 1895, 1898, and 1900.

Halley had golden blonde hair, while Olga had the auburn hair of her mother, showing deep red in the sunlight. Little Elsie had black hair. Bertha missed the Busch children and often brought her girls to play with them while Heinrich was at work. Halley, especially looked forward to these visits to the enormous house where she was sometimes given hand-me-down clothing, later passed on to her sisters. The Busch family invited the Melzl's to Christmas Eve where they engaged in the German tradition of looking for the pickle hidden in the tree, and to Easter for hunting for colorful eggs in the expansive yard.

When the girls were eight, ten, and thirteen, Heinrich bought them ice skates for Christmas. They learned to skate in the city park, with both parents giving pointers learned in their own youth. Perhaps because of these extended outdoor activities in the cold and wind, Elsie became ill with a sore throat and fever that lingered two weeks. She recovered for a month and then her symptoms returned.

Elsie complained of her joints aching and the fever came and went several times. Bertha mopped her brow with cool rags, and administered an elixir for pain from the apothecary that made her sleep so deeply Bertha checked to make sure she was breathing. Elsie gargled with hot salt water several times a day, but did not get better. Bertha wanted to call the doctor, but Heinrich thought it was an unnecessary expense. Elsie was diagnosed with Rheumatic Fever. It was a devastating prognosis likely to plague her throughout her life.

Her sisters brought home her lessons through that winter and spring, and when she felt well enough, she sat at the kitchen table to study while her mother baked bread and cooked the evening meal.

❧

W HEN ELSIE'S OLDER SISTER Halley was sixteen, she attracted the attention of a suitor named John Prichard. He saw her at the market where her mother had sent her for milk and flour.

"Good morning, Miss," John said and tipped his hat to her.

"Good morning, Sir," Halley replied, and smiled up into his handsome face.

"Today is so lovely, and you are so lovely, I could not help but say hello."

He walked beside her through the market, making pleasant conversation. When she indicated she was at her destination, he held open the door and waited while she made her purchases. They then continued to walk on together for several blocks sharing witty conversation.

They looked for each other on Saturday mornings after that and would walk together and talk. After several months of clandestine courting, Halley told her mother about her suitor, exclaiming John's good manners and handsomeness. Bertha advised Halley to invite John to meet her father.

When he came one evening, Heinrich questioned him about his upbringing and family. He was of Irish Catholic descent and recently arrived from New York, none of which set well with Heinrich, who knew a few Irishmen he did not like. Bertha listened to her eldest daughter continue to talk about her interest in John, but Heinrich would not listen to her.

One Saturday afternoon, Bertha turned from the sauerbraten she was basting, wiped her hands on her apron and sat down at the kitchen table with Halley. The other girls were outside hanging laundry providing some uncommon privacy in the house.

"I know that first love is powerful," she told Halley. "But you must honor your father's opinion. He does not trust this young man."

"Why? What does he know of him?" Halley asked.

"Your father asked around about him. Some of the people John associates with are unsavory."

"He is only newly arrived in St. Louis. He talks to many people, anyone who can help him find work. That does not make him a bad person."

"Perhaps not. But you should not encourage him any further."

One day a few months later, Halley did not return from the market at the expected time. She met John and they walked out into the fields south of the city. He was living in a boarding house and this was their first opportunity to be truly alone. John professed his love for her and his desire to marry her. She, in turn, gave herself to him willingly in a passionate tumble in the weeds.

It was almost dark when she arrived home with flushed cheeks and dirt on her skirt and bodice. Her father was furious. He told her harshly that she was forbidden from seeing John Prichard ever again. Later that evening Bertha sat on the edge of Halley's bed just before lights out and tried to explain to her daughter.

"Your father wants what is best for you. He does not want you to make a mistake that would cause you to have an unhappy life," she told Halley. "You also must think of your reputation and how it effects your father's standing in the community. Causing gossip is unwise."

"Mum, Dad should care what I want and how I feel. Why does he object to John so much?"

"I told you before. Your father has looked into that young man. He does not have a story that can be verified. He is a drifter. And he is seen with people who may be on the wrong side of the law."

"I do not believe it! Mother, I love him."

"My dear girl. I understand how you feel. There was a young man in our village that was keen to walk with me in the evenings. People in our village thought that our friend-ship would one-day lead to marriage. But then, my father decided it would be best for me to go to America. He made arrangements, bought my passage, and put me aboard a ship. I never even said goodbye to Hamish. It was hard, but it was for my father to decide what was best. I am glad to be here and thank him for choosing a better life for me."

Though Friedrich had let Bertha make the final decision, she did not share this information with Halley. It was better that Halley respect Heinrich as the authority. Bertha knew her husband did not have the same kind of affection for the girls that she had received from her own father.

A few weeks later, hat in hand, John came to the door and formally asked Heinrich for Halley's hand in marriage. Heinrich flatly said that he would never condone their marriage and that he was to leave Halley alone. He showed John the door and slammed it behind him.

Halley wept for several days. Bertha, Olga and Elsie all tried to console her without success. Despite her father, Halley continued to find alibis and places to meet John. Eventually, one of Heinrich's friends at work said he had seen Halley walking hand in hand with a young man. When he came home from the brewery, he walked directly to where Halley sat at the table and grabbed her by the hair. He pulled her to her feet and marched her down the hall, and slapped her hard across her face sending her reeling into her room. He slammed the door behind her. He had never raised a hand to his wife or children, but then he had never had any reason to be angry with them.

The following day Halley stood awkwardly in the kitchen doorway to speak to her mother. Her eye was black and the side of her face showed a purple bruise from her father's abuse.

"I am sorry mother. I know defying father has made him angry." Halley took a deep breath, swallowed hard and continued. "John was doing the right thing to ask for my hand. I am carrying his child."

Bertha stood and stared into her daughter's eyes for several moments gathering her words.

"But he did not do the right thing by laying with you out of wedlock. You have been very foolish," her mother said sternly. Then she closed her eyes and breathed deeply. When she opened them, tears spilled down her face. "You cannot even understand what you have brought down on yourself. You must gather your things, child, and leave before your father comes home. You have to leave for your safety, as well as that of your unborn baby. Heinrich will not bear this shame without repercussions. He will beat you and then shun you."

Bertha wiped away tears and her heart pounded as she helped her daughter pack a small satchel with clothes. Her mother gave her a narrow silver necklace with an angel charm that had been around her neck since she left Germany. It was a parting gift from her own mother when Bertha had left for America. They embraced and said a silent, tearful goodbye.

That evening, frightened of how Heinrich would react, Bertha gathered her courage and told him about the baby and that Halley was gone.

Heinrich paced the floor for an hour without saying a word. His unspoken rage hung in the air. The house was silent all evening. Before going to bed, he went to the family Bible and tore out the page with their names and dates of birth. The next day he took it to a bookbinder and asked him to sew a new page on the front. He picked up the Bible on his way home from work three days later. That evening, he sat at his desk and carefully transcribed each name and date from the page he had removed, omitting Halley. He then threw the original page into the fire. He instructed his family never to utter her name again. She would no longer exist. Bertha cried herself to sleep.

She confided in Lilly about the anger she felt toward her husband. Lilly was sympathetic but counseled her to try to forgive him. She needed to respect her husband even if they disagreed.

"You need to be strong, Bertha. Trust that God will look after Halley," Lilly advised her as they sat in the drawing room behind closed doors. "Focus on Olga and Elsie. They are at a vulnerable age."

Bertha tried several times over the next months to approach Heinrich about Halley. She told him they needed to make amends before John took Halley away where they might never find her. Each time Heinrich would shout and frighten Bertha. Eventually she stopped trying to reason with him. In fact, she stopped talking to him altogether unless it was necessary.

❦

IN 1911, BERTHA WENT back to work at the Busch home while Olga and Elsie were at school during the day. The Busch children she had raised were now having children of their own that they brought to the big house for lessons with Bertha.

Her girls, now eleven and thirteen, helped her by starting the evening meal when they were home from the public school, as well as baking bread and helping with the laundry on weekends.

This arduous task started at 7:00 a.m. Underclothes, white shirts, and aprons were washed every week. The bedding was rotated every other week, along with dark colored pants, skirts and dresses. Laundry was soaked and scrubbed on washboards, then put into boiling water on the stove with Lux laundry soap. They were then rinsed, the whites with bluing, run through a wringer, and hung to dry. The clothesline in the back yard served most of the year, but when it was raining or below freezing, clotheslines hung throughout the whole downstairs for the day.

Olga and Elsie would never dream of disappointing their father after witnessing his treatment of Halley. They never saw or heard of Halley again. The girls studied hard and earned good grades in school. When they were not helping their mother with chores, they both worked on quilts for their marriage trousseaus'. These were carefully pieced and sewn on a treadle machine, then hand quilted. Throughout their teen years, they worked on several quilts, embroidered bed linens, and knit coverlets.

When Olga was eighteen her father granted her marriage to Ben Thompson, a college graduate who was going on to dental school. They met at a dance and dated for six months before their engagement.

Olga and Elsie helped plan the church wedding and made Olga a sleeveless V-neck dress of cream-colored satin. A waist sash fell diagonally down to the mid-calf length. The church alter was decorated with flowing vines and white flowers gathered from the market stalls the morning of the wedding. Ben's parents paid for the flowers when Heinrich refused, calling them a waste of hard-earned money.

Elsie finished high school in 1918. She was small and thin, only five foot one inch. She wore her dark hair short, as was the fashion of the day. Her round face had a charming deep dimple on one side when she smiled. Uncertain what to do, she began offering tutoring for the children of the wealthy St. Louis families, following in her mother's path. With the girls grown, Bertha went back to live at the Busch home, leaving Elsie to look after Heinrich. Elsie felt sorry for her father. He seemed simply to not have the capacity to care for the feelings of others. She cooked for him and kept the house. She and Bertha kept their close relationship with weekend visits. As her mother had done, she kept a quiet relationship with her father. They both read in the evenings after dinner as the clock ticked on the wall. Elsie saved all of her money from tutoring hoping to go to college someday so she could teach at the high school level.

In 1921, with help from her influential employers, she received a partial scholarship from Missouri Valley College in Marshall City, Missouri. Along with her savings, it was enough to begin her teaching degree. Leaving her father's home was bitter sweet. She was excited to move on with her path to independence, but worried about her father. She knew he would remain isolated and though they spoke little, her presence provided some relief from his lonely life.

College was a balm for her soul. She enjoyed every aspect of challenging classes, the well-kept campus, and dormitory life. During school breaks, Elsie stayed at her father's house and visited with her mother at the Busch home. While at school she met Eddie Purcell their senior year.

They both had noticed each other previously, but did not actually meet until they shared a class in teaching methods. They sat near each other and one day he walked her to the library after class. They then began meeting routinely there to study.

Eddie played football for the MVC Vikings, giving him an attractive muscular physique. Like Elsie, he was also earning a teaching degree. Eddie was of Welsh descent and had been raised a protestant, which pleased Heinrich when Elsie told him of her suitor. He had also enlisted in the Navy and had served for four years, then returned home to finish high school. This spoke to Heinrich of his patriotism and commitment to education.

Eddie met Elsie outside her dormitory most days and walked her to her first class, each carrying a satchel full of books and notebooks.

"Will you be at the game on Saturday?" he asked. He was proudly wearing his orange Viking letter sweater with a purple V sewn on the front.

"Of course! I have not missed one of your games all season," she smiled at him warmly. She bought a pennant at the school store and waved it at all the games along with her roommate, Edna.

"I have been keeping up on news about the American Professional Football Association. The sport is going to be huge. Wait and see," Eddie told her.

"I hope you aren't thinking of giving up teaching to go play ball instead," Elsie teased.

"Well, a man can dream, right? But, no. I am committed to my chosen career."

"Me, too," Elsie said, as they climbed the stairs and he held the door open for her.

"Does that mean you plan to work instead of marry," he asked.

Elsie blushed at the mention of marriage. "No. I want it all. I don't think I will necessarily have to choose one or the other," she said. "That is if I find a husband who is supportive of the idea."

She glanced over at him as they walked down the hall. He was considering what she had said.

Finally, he responded, "Well maybe I can coach football after school if I marry someone who would allow it." With that, he gave her a broad grin, kissed her on the cheek and left her at her classroom door as he turned back down the hall to go to his own. He turned around twice and was pleased to see her still standing there looking at him.

Elsie was named May Queen of the college in 1924 just before they both graduated. Edna and the Domestic Arts Teacher, Miss Trumble, helped her make a dress to wear from fabric provided by the theater club. It was a long narrow white gown with a lace overlay and a flowing veil of sheer silk voile.

A ceremony and professional photo shoot preceded a student dinner and dance. Eddie and Elsie danced together most of the night and shared a long passionate kiss when they said goodnight on her dormitory doorsteps.

The night before June graduation, Eddie sat on those same steps with her hands in his.

"Elsie, I want to ask you something. We have been dating for almost a year now and I adore you. With school ending,

I cannot bear the thought of saying goodbye. If your parents agree, will you marry me?" He stared into her eyes holding his breath.

Elsie squeezed his hand. "Eddie, I would love to be your wife."

He broke into a huge smile and leaned over to kiss her, but before their lips touched, she said, "But…"

He leaned back in sudden alarm that she had already changed her mind.

"There is something about me I have not told you, which may influence how you feel," she began. "When I was young I was very sick and they said it was rheumatic fever. As I am sure you know, this damages the heart. My heart is not strong. It may shorten my life."

Eddie did not miss a beat, "I don't care. I mean, of course I care, but it does not deter me. I will cherish whatever time we share together." Then they shared a long slow romantic kiss, sealing their devotion to each other.

Heinrich and Bertha rode together on the train mostly in silence to attend the outdoor graduation. Eddie's parents were there and they all spent the afternoon together walking around the campus and sitting in the sunshine.

Eddie's parents had met Elsie previously at his football games. They thought she was charming. That evening, Heinrich and Bertha took the young couple out to dinner, where Eddie asked for their blessing to marry Elsie. They married later that summer in the same church as Olga and Ben. Elsie once again wore the May Queen gown and veil. The Busch's chef made the wedding cake for the reception, and Heinrich surprised everyone with Champaign.

Eddie found a teaching position in Keokuk, Iowa that fall. They rented a small apartment walking distance from campus and became pregnant with their first child. They worried about Elsie's health and Eddie begged her to rest as much as possible.

Then, when she was just two months from giving birth, her father died at the age of seventy. They took the train to St. Louis where the Busch family paid for his burial and simple headstone:

HEINRICH MELZL
1854 – 1926

Bertha, Olga, Ben, Elsie, and Eddie attended the brief graveside service. Afterwards they went to the Busch house for coffee with Lilly who was now eighty-two years old. Adolphus had died in 1913.

Lilly asked Bertha, "What do you want to do with the house? Do you want to go back and live there?"

"No. That house is not a happy place for me. It makes me sad to even cross the threshold," Bertha said in little more than a whisper. Then she looked up at Olga and then Elsie. "Perhaps either of you feel differently. Would you ever want to live there?"

Olga reached over and took Ben's hand waiting for him to reply. "No, we plan to move south into Oklahoma or Arkansas and establish a dental practice in a town that needs one. St. Louis is getting too big."

Elsie looked at Eddie and they both said simultaneously, "No." Eddie continued, "We plan to move where our teaching careers take us."

"I can have it sold for you, if you like," Lilly offered. "My agent will get you a fair price."

"Thank you. Your assistance with that would be greatly appreciated," Bertha said. "While everyone is here in town we will go there and see if there is anything worth keeping."

Elsie took dishes, pots and pans, and kitchen utensils. Olga and Elsie divided the bedding. Heinrich's clothing went to the church for charity. There was little else but the furniture, which they left behind. None of them wanted the family Bible. They left it on the shelf above the fireplace.

When the house sold, Lilly's agent opened a savings account in Bertha's name at the National Bank of Commerce in St. Louis with the proceeds.

Plantation One

PENOBSCOT RIVER, MAY, 1764: Seventeen-year-old Jacob was sent out by his father to hunt. Yesterday he brought home three rabbits and a grouse, but between his father and two older brothers that was all gone. Today he hoped for a deer at least. They had been living along the Penobscot River for three months now waiting for the supply ship that would bring settlers to work the land. Jacob's father, Jonathan Buck had been commissioned to survey six plantations in the region two years earlier. Now he was here with his three oldest sons, Jonathan Junior who was twenty-one, Garrison who was nineteen, and Jacob.

So far, they had established a small lumber mill that facilitated building a house for themselves and a store that would supply settlers once they arrived, along with the goods to stock the store. They had also built a dock out into the river. Even so, boats could only access the dock at high tide. When the tide was low, the river would have forty feet of deep mud between the shore and the water.

The land was not without people, but those who were there lived a rustic isolated life. They included the Penobscot Indians and various fur traders from Canada. Some spoke only French and Jonathan instructed his sons to be wary of people living around them in the forest. The nation was in a state of unrest with the British and French vying for territory on the largely unsettled continent.

Back home in Haverhill, Massachusetts, Jacob's mother was caring for his two younger sisters and one other brother. There had been three other children who died of smallpox before the age of five. His mother and younger siblings were expected to join them at the plantation as soon as the settlement was established, perhaps the following spring.

It was difficult to imagine them being here in this wild place. It would be some time before the settlement had the comforts afforded them in Haverhill. For now, everyone was on their own for safety and survival. Food had to be found every day. Each person had to ensure their own safety from wild animals, harsh weather and dangerous people. It was a lawless land without an organized militia. When the rest of the family arrived, these burdens would increase.

Jacob thought of the comfort his mother would provide by preparing the meals, tending to the house, and mending their worn clothing. But then he thought of the additional food that would have to be secured for all of them.

Jacob enjoyed hunting and foraging. He liked being alone in the woods. His rifle and marksmanship gave him a sense of purpose and responsibility that felt good. His thoughts wandered to a day when he would have a wife of his own and children to care for, but that prospect seemed a long ways off. They had so much to do to make this wild place safe and productive enough to sustain a community.

As Jacob followed a deer trail through the woods, he stopped when he heard a strange sound. It was melodious, not a birdcall he recognized. Then he realized it was someone whistling a tune.

He crept through the woods and stooped when he spotted a girl picking fiddlehead ferns. She seemed neither wary, nor cautious, and appeared deep in her own thoughts. As he watched, she turned in executing her task and he saw she was using a knife with an eighteen-inch blade to cut the ferns. She was clad in a patchwork tapestry of odd pieces of fabric and skins. Her bodice and skirt were of a small plaid, well worn and patched with other remnants of fabric. She wore a piece of fur over her shoulders in the early morning chill, and her feet were covered with boots made of animal skins held up by rawhide pieces tied at her ankles.

She finished her gathering and moved off into the woods in the opposite direction from Jacob's path. When he lost sight of her, he resumed his tracking down the trail. About three minutes later, an object from above knocked him flat on the ground face-first. Before he could catch his breath, a knee pinned him in the middle of his back, his wrist was wrenched up nearly to his shoulder blade and a knife dug into his throat.

The girl spoke French, which he did not understand, then switched to English with a deep French accent.

"What are you doing watching me?" she demanded.

Jacob swallowed hard, his heart pounding with adrenaline. "I did not mean to disturb you. I am just hunting for food."

"Why should I believe you?" she said through clenched teeth and wrenched his wrist up painfully high on his back.

"I don't know," he blurted out. "I mean you no harm. I am Jacob Buck. I am hunting for food for my family."

A few moments passed. She started to ease up the pressure on his pinned arm, but did not remove the knife from his throat. "I will let go of you, but if you move suddenly, I will gut you like a fish."

He nodded his head slightly acknowledging their agreement. She let go and stood back holding the knife out in front of her in a crouch as if ready to launch at him. He stood slowly, adjusted his rifle slung over his shoulder and brushed off the debris that clung to his clothes. They stared at each other. Her hair was a wild mass of curls that hung nearly to her waist and framed a long face with high cheekbones. Her wide eyes transfixed him. They were brilliant green with a turquoise rim around each iris. He could not tell her age, but guessed she might be a few years older than he was.

"You need not be frightened, Miss," he said gently. "I mean you no harm," he said again.

They stood for another moment. Then she slowly lowered her knife.

"What is your name?' he asked.

She stared at him some more, calculating her answer. Finally, she stood a bit taller and said, "Saidie."

"I am pleased to make your acquaintance, Saidie. What is your sir name?" he asked.

"I only have one name. Saidie," she said defensively.

He nodded. "My father and brothers live along the river. We are starting a settlement there."

She did not reply.

"I am following this deer trail hoping to bring home food," he said.

She stared into his eyes for an uncomfortable length of time. Then she motioned for him to follow her. She walked down the trail one hundred yards and then turned off into a thick wood. On the far side was a meadow with a large buck and four does. He silently kneeled and took his shot, hitting the buck in the chest. When he turned around the girl was gone.

The animal was too large for him to carry all of it. He quartered it and strapped the two hindquarters onto his back. When he returned to the partially finished house on the river, he left the meat for Garrison to cut up and went back to retrieve the rest. When he arrived at the kill site, only one of the front quarters remained.

By the time he got home, his father and older brother were there waiting to help with the butchering.

"Where did you lose the other front quarter, son," his father asked.

"It was gone when I returned," he answered. He did not mention the girl, though he was sure she took it. He did not know what to make of her, but he wanted to think it through for himself before telling anyone.

"Couldn't you see marks of it being dragged off," his oldest brother asked.

"Not really. The underbrush was thick," he answered evasively.

"Well, no matter," his father said. "You did well today. And most likely there is a grateful bear out there, too."

They ate a hearty supper of roasted meat, baked beans, and biscuits cooked in a Dutch oven on the woodstove they brought from Haverhill.

As the summer progressed, Jacob saw Saidie many more times. She found him in most instances, rather than the other way around, and he got the feeling she was watching him often as he hunted, cut wood, or foraged for berries. She never approached him when he was with his brothers or father, only when he was alone. She knew where the animals were many times and made hunting much easier. She also taught him about some of the edible mushrooms in the woods.

Finally, when they were picking berries one day, he asked her where her people were. She was always alone.

"I have no people. I had a mother and a sister but they died," she told him.

"How long ago," he asked.

"Two years now. I live alone. My mother taught me how to survive. How to kill game, what to eat, how to hide from other people."

"What about your father," he asked.

"No father," she said.

He continued to keep their friendship a secret from his family. He was attracted to her and did not want his brothers to know about her. Besides, he was unsure what his father would think. It was easier to keep it a secret.

It was early August before she trusted him enough to show him where she lived. It was deeply hidden in the woods, half of it was a cave and the other built of branches lashed together. She had a fire pit inside and a vent above that opened and closed.

Animal skins lined the floor and walls, and her bed was a pile of furs. She made him rabbit stew that day with wild greens and herbs she had collected. As she handed him a wooden bowl of the stew, their hands touched briefly. At that moment, their eyes locked and something passed between them. It was a sense of intimacy and safety. She had let him into her world and he was comfortable there. The stew was far better than what he and his brothers cooked.

It was a week later on a very warm day that she showed him a hidden pool of deep water in the shadows of the forest. She filled her gourds with the water to take back, then took off her boots and waded in the cool water. He watched her and then began to untie his bootlaces to join her. When his feet were free, he looked up to see her staring at him. She looked deep in thought. Then slowly she reached down to the laces on her bodice, untied them and pulled her dress over her head. She flung it up onto the rocks and dove into the cool clear water. He was astonished at her forwardness and delighted by her sheer nerve. He followed her lead, unburdening himself of his shirt and trousers and diving in. They swam, splashed, and laughed.

When they came out of the water, she stood and faced him completely naked, her lean lithe body dripping wet. She reached for her clothes, spread them on the ground in the sun, and lowered herself to her knees. He swallowed hard, hesitated, and then slowly sat down beside her. Their shoulders and thighs touched and they both leaned in simultaneously for a passionate kiss. They lay down in the sun and fumbled through the making of first love.

After that, they nearly always went to the pool or to her house to be together. They greeted each other with a kiss, and would hold hands as they walked through the woods. When they sat together on the creek bank fishing, they spoke without words, deep in their own intertwined thoughts of love, the first for each of them.

Finally, as the weather began to turn in September, he told his father about her. Jonathan had many questions that Jacob could not answer.

"Where did you meet this girl?" Jonathan asked.

"Out in the woods. She lives out there on her own. She is adept at providing for herself," Jacob said.

"How old is she?" his father asked.

"I don't know. I do not think she knows. She might be a little older than me is all," Jacob said.

"Is she a Puritan like us?"

"I don't think so. She has a French accent. Maybe her people were Catholics or Protestants," Jacob speculated. "Father, she is all alone. It seems the Christian thing to invite her into our community, or at least let her know she is safe with us. I believe we should protect her."

"Hmm. Do you? Well, bring her around to meet us at least. She should know not to fear us," Jonathan said.

"Thank you, Father. I will invite her next time I see her," Jacob said and smiled to himself as he turned away.

It was a week later on a chilly autumn day that he brought Saidie to their house on the river. It was largely completed now and stood two stories, with precious glass windows that had come on the supply ship. There were more settlers arriving each month and they passed people on the two-track road that ran through what would become a town.

Everyone stared at the girl dressed like a gypsy with her wild hair billowing around her in the wind. He showed her into their house and Saidie stood and stared around and up at the ceiling and up the stairs. Then she turned her gaze to Jonathan.

"Welcome, Miss. Please have a seat," Jonathan said gesturing to a chair at the table. "May we offer you a cup of tea?"

"No, thank you," she said warily.

"Jacob tells me you live alone in the woods. How extraordinary," he began. She did not reply. "Did your mother raise you as a Christian?"

She stared at him. Then finally, she blurted out, "My mother had little use for such conventions. She raised my sister and me to take care of ourselves and survive. She came from Montreal."

"I see," he said and looked at Jacob meaningfully. "Are you quite alright in your current situation? Will you be able to survive in the woods if we have a harsh winter? You could come live closer to the plantation headquarters. It could give you some sense of safety."

"I live in the house my mother made. It is fine," she answered.

Jonathan continued chatting on for some time about his plans for the plantation and the building of a community that was underway. She listened mostly in silence, nodding her head occasionally. When he ran out of things to say, they bid farewell, he saying he was pleased to meet her, her saying nothing much.

Jacob walked her back down the road, with his father watching from the window. He saw Jacob reach over and pull her close and she reciprocated by putting her arm around his waist. They walked on close together, and Jonathan heaved a great sigh.

When Jacob returned in the evening, Jonathan said, "Son, that girl is a wild thing. It is kind of you to befriend her, but you must remember who you are. You cannot fall for a girl like that no matter how pretty she is. Do you understand?"

Jacob sat down, leaned forward in his chair and placed his head in his hands staring down at the floor. The clock ticked on the wall.

"Jacob. Your mother has found a lovely girl in Haverhill that she thinks would be a good match for you. She wrote to me about her. Her name is Martha. She is a Puritan and comes from a good family," Jonathan said gently.

"Father, Saidie has no one. And she knows so much about these woods and the animals and plants. She could teach us all a lot," Jacob said.

"I have no doubt she could. Those qualities would make her a good match for a fur trader. But that does not make her a potential wife for you," he said sternly.

"It is too late, father. We are in love with each other," Jacob said defiantly.

"No. No, you are not. You are young and foolish. You need to follow my guidance. I know what is best for you," Jonathan said.

Jacob said nothing. He went to bed that night feeling desperate to be with Saidie. He slept restlessly and dreamed that they ran away together. He woke feeling sick to his stomach with the anguish of his situation.

꩜

A FTER FIVE DAYS PASSED with no sign of her, he went to her house in the forest, but she was not there. He waited for her until the sun was setting, then went home beginning to worry. The fireplace had been warm at her house, so he knew she was around somewhere. He decided he would have to wait for her to come find him as she had so many times. After a week, she silently joined him as he walked a path tracking game. He stopped and faced her and she reached up and touched his face. She looked sad. He was worried. They walked on for thirty minutes until they reached a hilltop with a view of the valley below. He sat on a rock to rest and she sat beside him. He reached for her hand.

"Your father does not like me," she said.

"No, it is not that he does not like you, Saidie. My father is a kind, caring person," he said. After a long pause, he tried to explain. "My father has strong ideas about the life I will lead. He and my mother want me to marry a certain type of girl."

"Not a half-breed French Indian who lives in the woods?" she said sarcastically.

He sighed heavily and ran his fingers through his hair. "My father has no prejudice toward French or Indian people. But he does want me to marry a girl from a Puritan family, raised in a proper English household."

"Is the choice not yours?" she asked.

"If I do not follow my father's counsel then he will make an example of me for my brothers. I do not know exactly what he would do, but I fear it would be unpleasant for both you and me."

"I see. What will you do then?" she asked.

They sat for a long time. He struggled with his emotions and words. She waited.

When the sun started to set, she stood up, leaned over and kissed him gently on the lips, then slowly walked off toward her home. Jacob wept.

❧

THEY DID NOT SEE each other until winter set in and the ground was covered with snow and ice. Having found relief from her loneliness over the summer, she was distressed to be alone once again. She decided she could not forget Jacob without trying one more time. She decided to go talk to his father. In the dim afternoon light, she made her way into the settlement. She saw Jonathan moving equipment into a buckboard wagon and approached him.

He stopped working and tipped his hat to her. "Good day, Saidie. How are you fairing in this cold weather? Everything alright?"

"Yes, thank you for asking. I was wondering if I might speak to you."

"Of course. We can go to the house. The boys are out working on one of the new houses," he said.

They walked the short distance to the house and he closed the door behind them. As before, they sat at the table.

"How may I help you, Saidie?" he asked kindly.

She mustered her best manners and spoke carefully enunciating each word clearly. "Sir, I know that you do not find me suitable for Jacob. But, I am in love with him. My appearance is because of my circumstances. These clothes are what I have, not who I am. I can be the sort of daughter-in-law you want to have. My mother taught me to read and write. I am not ignorant."

They sat quietly for a moment.

Then he said gently, "I am so sorry that I cannot approve your marriage to my son. You must understand that my wife has found him a girl to marry. She will be bringing her here in the spring. I am sure that you will find another young man. There are many settlers coming, bringing their families. If you need help this winter with food or shelter, call on me. I am at your service. But I cannot condone you seeing my son. Do you understand?"

Tears filled her eyes despite her pride. She rose and turned to leave without further conversation.

In December, a horrible storm came down from the northeast. The wind howled and it rained ice, and then snowed for days. Then the temperature dropped to 20 below zero.

Jacob could not help himself. He set off through the deep drifts to check on Saidie. He arrived half-frozen at her home to find her frostbitten and deranged with a high fever. He made a fire to warm them both, then set about making a sled to bring her to the settlement. He cut balsam boughs and lashed them together, then fashioned a harness out of rawhide straps Saidie had made for future use. He laid her on the sled and covered her with furs. It was nearly midnight when he arrived back home.

They made a bed for her and dosed her with laudanum. Both her feet had been badly frostbitten. One appeared to be recovering circulation and the color was getting better each day. The other was black. Jacob spooned hot tea and broth into her mouth and moped her brow with cool rags. Saidie's fever continued to rage. Jacob did not want to leave her side, but the business of survival continued unabated. He would be out hunting for hours, only to return and find her despondent. He would rouse her, feed her, stroke her hair and speak softly to her through the evening. He feared she was dying.

Jonathan and his brothers looked on and whispered their worst fears when out of hearing of the couple.

"We have to remove her foot or she will die of gangrene," Jonathan declared to his older sons. "This will be difficult. But there is no other way. We have to try and save her life."

He broke the news to Jacob in a gentle voice as they sat at the table after supper. Jacob sat with his head in his hands, elbows on the table. Tears dripped down his arms. Jonathan waited for his son to speak.

"I would do anything to try and save her, Father."

"Good. That is the Christian thing to do. But you do not need to help. If you wish, your brothers and I will do it," Jonathan told him.

"No. I need to be there for her," Jacob said decisively.

It was a gruesome affair. They gave her the last of their laudanum. Garrison stood above her head and held down her shoulders. The younger Jonathan held down her other leg, and they strapped the leg to be amputated to the bed rail. Jacob held her hands tight in his and gazed into her ashen face. Jonathan sawed the leg off with a bone saw used for butchering deer. They worked together to stitch up the arteries and veins and sewed the gaping wound closed. Jacob ran outside to vomit twice during the procedure.

She had lost much blood and was pale and weak. Her fever continued unabated. It was five days later that she became lucid and realized the full extent of what had happened. She screamed and cursed Jonathan and told him she would haunt him forever for mutilating her body and for denying her the love of his son. She declared that he had killed her.

Jonathan was beside himself. He did his very best to save her, but in her deranged state, she did not believe him. After her angry outburst, she became calm. Her eyes were glassy as she gazed into Jacob's eyes. He sat beside her listening to her last wishes. She reached into a pocket, took out an amethyst amulet, and placed it in Jacob's hand.

"This is to remember me, Jacob. To remember how much I loved you. My mother gave it to me just before she died. She said it can influence outcomes, but must be used wisely. Do not underestimate its power."

He closed his hand over the charm and saw the light leave her eyes. She was gone. Adding to the horror of her death was the unforgiving frozen land that could not be penetrated to receive her body. Jonathan said they would need to burn the body. Jacob worked with his father and brothers to build a pyre in the woods. Then he wrapped her in a blanket and carried her body to the place.

Jonathan said a brief prayer. "Heavenly Father, please receive the soul of this young woman into your kingdom where she can rest from the burdens of her life in the rugged place. Forgive us for failing to save her precious life. Amen."

He used a lit torch to set the kindling afire and the flames rose to engulf her shroud.

When spring finally came, Jacob visited her house. There was little to inform anyone of who she had been. Just the few utilitarian things she used to survive. He realized the amulet she had given him was her only treasure. He kept it in his pocket. He carved a headstone and placed it at the place where her body transformed to ashes. It read simply:

BELOVED SAIDIE
TAKEN 1764

Out of the Pool Hall

T HE BIRTH OF ELSIE's first child in August 1926 was difficult, requiring a longer than usual recovery. She was
weak for several months afterwards. Their son, Bret, was
a healthy boy gaining weight on schedule according to the
doctor. He grew to be a bright sweet boy, full of energy.
His favorite toy was a wooden sword used in mock battles
against his other toys. He had a curious nature and tried
his parents' patience with experimental activities, such as
the time he dropped a rock in his mother's silk stocking
and whipped it around his head like a lasso. By the time
his mother discovered him in the backyard, the precious,
expensive stocking was nearly ten feet long.

During summers off from teaching, Eddie enrolled in
graduate school at University of Iowa studying Wildlife Conservation. He was passionate about all aspects of the conservation movement and its integration with agricultural
management. Through the program, he met like-minded
people and learned about educational camps to teach children in their early years about the importance of caring

for nature. When his degree was finished, he planned to pursue involvement in such camps during summer breaks from teaching.

Bret started school in the trough of the Great Depression. Elsie took a teaching job at his grade school to bring in more money. With the double income, the parents invested in a bank repossessed 1920 Ford Model T. Their little family and their career plans were all coming together despite the state of the nation. The dust bowl intensified Eddie's commitment to the intertwined relationship between nature and industrial agriculture. He felt he was exactly where he needed to be in his life, marriage, and education.

That is when little Bret suddenly became ill. He saw three doctors over two months before diagnosed with bone tuberculosis. The collaborating doctors traced the disease to unpasteurized milk sold at the Keokuk market. The infection manifested in his ankle. Elsie had to quit her job to care for him.

For ten months, his parents made the arduous journey to Providence Hospital in Kansas City by car, nineteen times in all weather. The car could only go 40 miles an hour, so the trip took six and a half to seven hours. There the doctors treated Bret with caustic medicines and several surgeries to remove affected parts of his anklebone. He slept on the way home, blankets piled over him in the back seat of the drafty car. Many times his father had to go to work after driving all night to get them home.

Elsie worried incessantly. She feared for her son, but also for her husband. He was stretched too thin teaching and studying for his degree, driving to Kansas City, and keeping the car in working order. Besides occasionally helping him grade tests and papers late into the night, she did not know how to help him. She corresponded with his mother to keep her up to date since Eddie had no time to spare for letter writing. The replies soothed her in the sharing of concerns.

Finally, a time came when the doctors declared Bret's full recovery. Though the damaged ankle would plague him throughout his life, they could all move on with the business of everyday living.

In 1936, Eddie accepted a teaching position in Dallas, Texas, with better pay and football coaching duties. That year outlaws Bonnie Parker and Clyde Barrows, along with their gang, as well as "Pretty Boy" Floyd were dominating the news. Ten-year-old Bret was fascinated with the horrifying progress of the outlaws and the young family wondered if they had wandered too far into a lawless land. Elsie provided private tutoring for students in their home. Later that year, she gave birth to another boy. The birth was easier this time and together Eddie and Elsie decided to have a third child before she returned to her career path in education.

Dallas was a city of 300,000 people in the 1930s. By the time Bret was thirteen, he and his friend Scobey were allowed to take the bus downtown to go to the movie theater. Bret never got tired of Scobey exclaiming, "My eyes!" when the lights went down for the film to start. Afterwards they would loaf around, window shop or get a treat at the drug store soda fountain. Though they never encountered any trouble, Eddie and Elsie were apprehensive about raising a family in a place where Italian mobsters stalked by the FBI ran nightclubs, gambling joints, prostitution rings and narcotics. The nefarious Piranio family was well known. The boys were cautioned to stay on the main streets and out of the pool halls. This became the boys' favorite joke. Whatever they decided to do for the day, one or both of them would intone, "It'll keep us out of the pool hall."

Boredom led the friends to enter a church one day when they saw the door propped open to let in the breeze. Eddie and Elsie were not churchgoers and Bret had never so much as stepped inside one. Scobey said he had been to a wedding in one when he was younger. They were warmly greeted by the pastor who told them they were always welcome. They wandered through the interior enjoying the vaulted ceilings, stained glass windows and statues. When they told their parents about this discovery, visiting churches was added to their list of safe things to do downtown. Thus began a routine of not only touring the buildings, but sitting in the pews to escape the heat outside, and occasionally even attending a service. They liked the music and singing, especially when there was a well-practiced choir. Inspired, Bret joined the choir at school. These forays also led to conversations between them about God.

Bret asked Scobey if he thought they had a better chance of going to heaven if they went to more church services.

"I don't know, maybe," said Scobey. "But does it matter which one? If we join all the churches, we might get free passes to heaven for our parents, too."

Bret laughed. "That would be swell. Then next time we get into trouble, we can tell them we got them into heaven, and they would have to forgive us."

They were generally good kids, but one time Scobey's mother caught them smoking cigarettes lifted from her purse. "They will stunt your growth. You aren't old enough to smoke," she admonished them. "And thieving them from my purse makes it even worse."

Bret's father was a smoker though Elsie did not approve of it. Bret liked the smell of the rich tobacco and saw how smoking helped his father relax in the evening. He also saw the older kids smoking and thought it would make him look mature to have a pack in his shirt pocket.

Bret and Scobey started skipping the soda fountain to buy cigarettes instead. Then they would find an out-of-the-way spot to practice smoking. There was much coughing and they went home with sore throats.

One afternoon when they were walking around in downtown Dallas, they happened by a saddle-making shop. They stood looking through the window for the longest time watching a man on the other side using leather stamps to emboss the leather of a saddle. Another man approached the shop and saw the boys enthralled expressions and invited them inside. He might have been the owner of the shop or just another employee but he showed the boys around and told them how saddles were made. Before they knew it, they had been there for over an hour and it was time to head toward home. On the bus back home, Bret declared that he wanted to make his very own saddle someday.

The friends said goodbye each summer when Bret left with his father to go to St. Johns Academy in Delafield, Wisconsin. Eddie was the head counselor there, which gave Bret free enrollment. The camp on Lake Geneva was a wonderful reprieve from the Texas heat. Structured days were filled with swimming lessons, hiking, bird watching, archery, animal tracking, insect identification, horseback riding and target shooting. In the evenings, there were campfires, cookouts, storytelling, star viewing, and sometimes singing. As Bret grew and learned the lessons again each summer, he soon became a junior counselor himself.

Eddie raised Bret to appreciate the value of staying busy. There was always something new to learn to better yourself and by extension make the world a better place. Eddie demonstrated this through his own commitment to teaching at the camp every summer and leading boy scouts back in Dallas. Boys needed guidance and he hoped he could help to instill honorable values of patriotism, hard work, honesty, and service to others. Eddie's influence shaped Bret into a person with an active curious mind and a constant pursuit of personal growth. How this manifested itself sometimes surprised everyone, including Bret.

During these years, Bret liked the horses best. They were brought to the camp each summer from a ranch a few miles away. He would spend idle hours learning their quirks, grooming them and keeping them calm for the younger children to ride. Rubbing oil into the gear to soften and weatherproof it was one of his meditative joys. He also was a good marksman. He practiced shooting at camp and at home with his Dad. They cleaned the guns and watched each other practice the skill of stillness without so much as a breath to take the perfect shot.

One year the kids came up with an elaborate story about the camp being haunted. Bret at age fifteen took no stock in such things, but had to endure the younger kids speculating in whispers from their beds after lights out. The alleged haunting was primarily focused on the kitchen structure, which they all had to pass by on the way to the outhouse. Reported noises from inside including thumping, growling, and squeaking sounds. Finally, Bret decided to see this all to some conclusion and agreed to go with the six boys from their Bunkhouse B, ages ten through twelve. Late on a moonless night, they stumbled through the dark to the site of the frightening alleged commotion.

Bret held a flashlight and the rest trailed behind ready to escape back to safety as needed. They peered under the structure built on pilings, shined the light into all the windows, and even checked the slanted roof that was near the ground on the uphill side. They tried the door handle and it was locked as usual. An owl flew low over their heads and startled them, but they neither saw nor heard anything out of the ordinary.

"Satisfied?" Bret whispered. No one replied. They all traipsed back to their beds and Bret hoped that would be the end of it.

Two nights later, one of the boys named Kevin reported that a boy in Bunkhouse C had seen something move inside the window when he went by the previous night just before dawn. Bret spoke with Calvin who was the counselor from that bunkhouse about it.

"This is tiresome. I think it is just their imaginations, but it scares the younger boys," Bret said to Calvin.

"Maybe you and I should do a stakeout," Calvin suggested. "We can sit up and see what happens."

They chose a night when they knew the following day would include free time during which they could grab a nap to catch up on lost sleep. When the campers were asleep, they both slipped out and met at the kitchen building. Bret had cigarettes and they smoked while they talked in whispers.

"Hey, did you see the nurse's daughter today? Her name is Sarah. She looks like she is about our age," Calvin said.

"Oh, yeh! How could I miss her? She is really pretty," Bret replied.

"I hope she comes with her mother more times," sighed Calvin.

The nurse, Mrs. Barker, was there most days and on call for emergencies the rest of the time. The boys speculated that to be on call she must live close by.

"Next time Sarah comes, would you punch me or something so I can have an excuse to go to the nurse's station?" Calvin asked.

Bret snickered, "No, then I would be in trouble. But I would gladly push you over a cliff on the next hike."

"You are a true friend, Bret."

The truth was that Bret had his eye on Sarah and thought he would need to find a way to talk to her before Calvin. She had long thick dark brown hair, a slim waist and long legs. She was a real head-turner.

Just then as they were both lost in thought about Sarah, a thump came from the other side of the wall they were leaning against. They both sat up straight and listened. A shiver ran down Bret's spine. Calvin held his breath. A few minutes later just as they started to relax a bit, they heard the floor creak inside. The boys silently moved around to the front of the small building to the only entrance door. They stood in the dark and waited. But nothing more happened.

"Should we look inside?" Calvin asked.

"I guess we have to now," Bret replied.

They walked side by side slowly and quietly up the two steps to the door and tried the handle. It was locked. They walked silently around to one of the windows, pointed their flashlights in and turned them on simultaneously.

There was nothing but pots, pans, and shelves with canned goods. Nothing moved. They did the same in the other two windows. Nothing to see.

They walked back toward the bunkhouses, dumbfounded.

"Well, I wanted to put the boys' minds at ease. But now I don't know what to tell them," Bret whispered.

"Let's keep this little outing between us. Tell me if you hear any more rumors," Calvin whispered back.

"Will do. Sleep tight."

"Yeh, right," Calvin replied.

Bret lay awake for another hour trying to sort out what would be making the kitchen disturbance. He did not believe in ghosts and was determined to find the cause. The next day, while the rest of the camp was on leisure time in the afternoon, Bret went and found Calvin lounging in his bunk.

"Come on, get up," Bret said. "Let's go crawl under the kitchen building and look around. We can also talk to the cook."

"About what?" asked one of the younger boys who just woke up from a nap.

"Not for your ears, little friend," Calvin told him.

They walked over to the kitchen where the screen door was closed but they could clearly see Mrs. Wither stirring a huge pot of something that smelled like beef stew on the cook stove.

"Excuse me, Ma'am. May we have a moment," asked Bret.

Mrs. Wither turned her stout body toward them and wiped her hands on her apron. "No snacks in between meals, boys," she said and picked up a large chopping knife to prepare the heap of vegetables on the table.

"Yes, Ma'am. We know the rules. We just wanted to ask you if you found anything unusual in here this morning. We thought we heard a noise from inside and wondered if a varmint had gotten in," Bret explained.

"No. I can't think of anything odd or out of place. It sounds like the old ghost stories are circulating again?" she asked.

"Well, yes. That, too," Bret said. "How did you hear about it? That is if you don't mind my asking."

"And why do you say 'old,'" Calvin added.

Mrs. Wither scoffed. She kept chopping as the boys watched her through the screened door.

"This camp began in 1884, but the site has long been used for a hunting camp way before that," she told them. "My husband came here when he was a boy, about your age. He told stories about odd things happening. He said once they all heard a scream in the night coming from the woods. The next morning they looked for tracks to try to explain it. The scream did not sound like a deer or rabbit being killed. They said it sounded more like a person, a large man. But there were no tracks," She told them. "This building we use for a kitchen is the oldest of the cabins that were here from way back."

"So what do you think?" Bret asked her.

"I have been cooking here in the summer for four years. Before that, we used to hike up here in the winter to ice skate on the lake. We would build a fire next to this cabin for a wind shelter. I have never heard or seen anything out of the ordinary," she told them.

"Thank you, Ma'am." Said Bret. "Would you mind if we crawled underneath the building just to see if there are any holes that animals might be using to get inside."

"Fine with me. Be careful of snakes and spiders under there," she cautioned. "Today is the nurse's day off."

"We will be careful," Bret assured her.

They went around to the side where the floor was the highest off the ground. Bret crawled through and Calvin followed. There was only enough room for them to lay on their stomachs and raise their heads just enough to look up at the floor above. Batting away spider webs and trying not to breathe in too much dust, they shined their flashlights in all the corners. There were a few small holes and gaps along the edges, but they seemed more conducive to attracting mice than anything bigger. They crawled out and tried to dust themselves off without much success.

A few days later while leading archery practice, Bret saw Mrs. Barker's car pull in and was excited to see that Sarah was with her. When practice ended, Bret put away the equipment while everyone else headed out for a hike.

He went about various chores while keeping an eye on the nurse's cabin for any glimpse of Sarah. When she came out to sit on the porch in the sun, he gathered his nerve and approached her.

"Do you mind if I join you," he asked.

She looked up from daydreaming a bit startled. "Of course. I mean yes. I mean no, I don't mind," they both smiled at the obvious embarrassment and shyness.

"My name is Bret."

"I'm Sarah."

"Pleased to meet you," Bret said

"You as well. I mean I am pleased to meet you as well," Sarah blurted.

They both smiled some more and looked out at the lake.

"Do you like to come help your mother with her nursing duties?" Bret asked.

"She doesn't really need any help. Sometimes she has me check the supplies, or make notes in the log about kids that come in with scraped knees or bee stings," she answered. "But mostly I come with her just for something to do. It's cooler here by the lake than in town."

They sat in awkward silence for some time until Bret thought of something to say. "The kids like to talk about how this place is haunted. You ever hear anything about that?"

"Oh, yeh. Everyone in town has heard the stories. You believe it?" she asked.

"No, I don't believe in ghosts. But I do believe there are weird things that people hear and see. I wish I knew the cause so I could assure the kids not to be scared."

"Being scared is part of the experience of going to summer camp. They probably wouldn't even like it here if they didn't have ghost tales to take back to school in the fall."

This was so reasonable Bret suddenly lost interest in finding an answer. Sitting and talking to Sarah was more fascinating than solving mysteries.

As the weeks passed, Bret found several more times to see Sarah. He did not tell Calvin about this, until they were seen returning from a walk down by the lake.

"You sneak!" Calvin exclaimed in mock anger. "And all this time I thought you were my friend."

Bret laughed. "Sorry buddy. First come, first served. Just kidding. She is really nice and we are just getting to know each other. Besides, I am way better looking than you."

Calvin punched him in the arm with a grin and set off to get the fishing gear ready for the kids.

When camp was drawing to a close, Bret and Sarah exchanged addresses and promised to write to each other. Bret also gave his address to Calvin, but Calvin said he was not a letter writer.

"How about I write to you only if something really big happens, like I become captain of the football team and have a cheerleader for a girlfriend," Calvin offered.

"Okay. I won't hold my breath," Bret told him. They shook hands and saluted each other farewell, all the while grinning ear to ear.

It was a few months before Bret sat down with pen and paper to write a letter to Sarah. He had never written a letter before, which is why he had been procrastinating. Finally, he started and decided it was not really all that hard.

November 19, 1939
Dear Sarah,

I apologize for taking so long to write. I was only back home for a week before school started. My friend Scobey and I spent that last week of our summer break fishing every evening and catching up. He found a job while I was in Wisconsin sacking groceries at the neighborhood market. They said he could keep working Saturdays once school started. This makes me think I should look for a job here, too.

When school started, I found out that we had a new music teacher, Mrs. Wilson. I joined the choir and also go over to her house sometimes to sing with her kids, Becky and Robert. She is teaching us how to sing in harmony. Becky is a soprano and Robert and I are tenors. We have a good time together. Mrs. Wilson is concerned that I have been smoking cigarettes. She says it is not good for my voice. Now that I am sixteen my Dad said it is okay.

I joined ROTC and get to practice my shooting during school time. I also am taking wood shop and making my mother a cedar chest for Christmas. It has inlaid designs, which take a lot of extra time. I stay after at school to work on it. My great-grandfather was a cabinetmaker in Germany. Maybe I inherited his talent.

I sure do miss our walks together. I hope you are doing well in school and that you will write back to me.

Your friend,
Bret

The next summer they were back at camp in Wisconsin. Calvin did not come and it occurred to Bret that this might be his last summer there as college loomed ahead with other opportunities. Sarah came by the second week of camp and they fell into their old companionable friendship. She had written twice to his one letter and he was admonished for it. He apologized and promised to do better in the future.

On one of their walks by the lake Sarah told Bret that her cousins had visited at Christmas time and there was a great snowstorm. After being indoors for too many days, she and her cousins ventured out on snowshoes to the camp. It was all closed down for the holiday. The road had not even been plowed.

"It was so beautiful and peaceful up here with no one around," she told him. "We saw a Snowy Owl and an ermine. I think the ermine was spending the winter under the cook-house. He looked like a ghost so I thought you might want to know I solved the mystery."

"Oh, that's just swell. An ermine? Okay, that is what I will tell the kids when they have nightmares," he said. "It's better than having nothing to offer."

"I would think so," and she smiled warmly.

Bret picked up a rock and skipped it across the water. "I love coming here each summer. My Dad says that if young people are not taught to appreciate places like this, someday they will all be gone. There will be too many people in the world and nature will be swallowed up by cities."

"That would take a lot of people. The world is a big place," she said.

"Believe it," he said with conviction. "My Dad is one of the smartest men I ever met. If he says it, I believe it."

～❦～

WHEN THE JAPANESE ATTACKED Pearl Harbor in December 1941 triggering the United States entry into World War II, Bret and many of his classmates shared the fury of the country and wanted to enlist. At sixteen, he was too young. He heard about kids in the next grade up who were seventeen and able to enlist with their parent's permission. As soon as he heard about this, he went home to talk to his parents about it.

"Son, you are a good American. We have to fight for our freedom and your instinct to join the war is noble," Eddie told him. "Hopefully this war will be over soon now that the US has entered it, but if it is still going when you turn seventeen, and if you still want to, we will give our permission."

This made Bret feel like they respected him as the man he was becoming.

"What branch do you think I should join?" Bret asked.

"Well, you know I served in the Navy. I think a lot of this war will be at sea and our country has superior ships," Eddie said thoughtfully.

"Then that is where I want to be," he told his father.

"You also have to remember that your ankle would likely disqualify you for the Army or Marines. The Navy is your best bet for getting past the entry physical," Eddie told him.

In Bret's excitement, he had not even thought about his ankle. Now he was a little worried about being rejected.

"I am proud of you, son. Always have been. Always will be," Eddie said as he reached over and shook Bret's hand, bringing a tear to Elsie's eyes.

❧

B RET KNEW THIS WOULD be his last summer in Wisconsin. He wanted to use the time to get in the best physical shape he could in preparation for his military physical. He focused on his marksmanship and upper body strength. He worked on archery and swimming in his time off to build his core, chest, and arm muscles. But when Sarah was around, he spent as much time with her as possible. When it was time to say goodbye, he asked her for a parting kiss.

"Well, you are likely going off to war to be a soldier, so how can I deny this request," she said with a smile, and kissed him right on the lips much to his delight. Once again, they both promised to write.

August 20, 1942
Dear Sarah,
I enlisted in the Navy today! As you know, I was worried they would disqualify me because of my ankle. The doctor said I probably would have been denied in peace times, but because the US is in danger, they need all the men they can get. But what really helped was a letter from my ROTC commanding officer vouching for my marksmanship.
I will be trained as a gunner on a merchant marine ship.

They took a group picture of all us new recruits. There must have been five hundred of us. Everyone is ready to fight for our freedom.

I will write and tell you all about being in the Navy. I wish I could get just one more kiss before I ship out. Please write back.

Your friend,
Bret

He was assigned to a ship that supplied the South Pacific with lumber from the US west coast to rebuild docks destroyed in the bombing. The ship returned with goods from India. It took some time to get used to sleeping in a hammock that rocked counter to the ship's rocking. Every now and then storms made the hammocks rock too much so someone would fall out in the middle of the night.

Fresh water was a valuable commodity on the ship. Each man could have two showers a week on a set schedule. Guards stood outside the shower stall to monitor water usage. They were instructed repeatedly to "Get wet. Turn the water off to soap up. Rinse fast." Those that did not embrace the rules were hauled out even with soap in their eyes. No mercy.

The mysterious culture of India fascinated him. For his shipmates, shore leave meant drinking and seeking women for hire, a commodity in ample supply where poverty drove desperation. Bret spent his time off writing to his mother and Sarah. When he took shore leave, it was to explore. They anchored in ports in India, Hawaii, California, Oregon, and Washington.

January 1, 1943

Dear Mom,

India is different from anything you can imagine. The people are either well-to-do or living in so much poverty it is disturbing. They live by the Hindu caste system. Whatever class you are born into that is your lot in life. You cannot rise above your station through hard work like in our country.

When we arrived, we could see a lot of smoke down the beach from where we anchored. My commanding officer told me it was the place they burned the dead. He said that in all these port cities there is no place and no money for burying people. The bodies are brought down to the beach, laid on pyres and set on fire to burn. So strange to think of.

I went ashore and found a bookstore where I bought a book of poems by Rudyard Kipling. His poetry brings this strange culture to life beautifully. You can maybe find his writings at the library. If not, I will share this book with you when I return.

I saw a postcard with a photo of the Taj Mahal. I want to take the train there, but am advised it is dangerous. The people are so desperate; they will kill you to steal your shoes. I cannot get anyone interested in going with me for safety. My shipmates come back late from shore leave and fall in bed dead drunk. Sometimes they do not return at all until we are ready to pull anchor. I will try to get a shipmate to come with me next time we are in this port.

I hope you are not spending time worrying about me. We have not seen any action. I feel relatively safe compared to what I see in the news in other places.

Please tell Dad and the boys hi for me. I miss you all.
Your son,
Bret

Life out at sea was not without peril even when the enemy was nowhere nearby. Newspapers reported the devastation caused by a Typhoon in the Philippine Sea in December 1944. Three U.S destroyers capsized and sank killing over 790 people. In addition, many other ships suffered damage and aircraft swept from decks into the sea.

Bret sent a note to his parents that arrived in mid-January 1945.

December 25, 1944
Dear Mom and Dad,
I imagine you were concerned when you heard about the ships sinking in the big storm. Our ship was further south and east of the worst of it, but the seas were very rough. The twenty-foot-high waves tossed us around like a toy boat. No one slept that night, but we are all fine. I wish I were with all of you this Christmas Day. Today, all I can think about is all the families who are mourning sons, husbands, and fathers lost senselessly, not in valiantly fighting for freedom, but in that damned storm.

I will be discharged soon, probably later this year.
Bret

Oklahoma

B RET WAS HONORABLY DISCHARGED from the Navy in 1945 and returned bearing carved wooden elephants with ivory tusks for his mother. By this time, his parents and two young brothers had moved to Haileyville, Oklahoma, to be near Olga and Ben. Ben had opened his dental practice in nearby McAlester, and had been trying to coax Eddie and Elsie to move to Oklahoma. McAlester had grown significantly as a railroad and coal mining town. Prominent rail lines intersected with the *Missouri, Kansas, and Texas Railroad* running north south and the *Rock Island Line* running east west. McAlester had a large railroad station, foundry, brick making plants and an eleven story prestigious Renaissance-Sullivanesque style Aldridge Hotel on Grand Avenue. It was the county seat and site of the state penitentiary that hosted a wildly popular annual prison rodeo.

Ben's practice was upstairs in a building he had purchased down the street from the showpiece hotel and half a block off Main Street. A mercantile rented the lower floor. Ben and Olga lived in a small Victorian house they had purchased on the hill across the tracks and just west of the edge of town. They shared a close and loving marriage, despite their unfortunate discovery that they could not have children. Olga raised birds in their large yard: guinea hens, geese, ducks, chickens, turkeys.

Elsie and Eddie both had found positions at the Haileyville High School ten miles east of McAlester. Eddie taught math and science and coached football, while Elsie taught English at the two-story brick school. They bought a small one-story, three-bedroom house a few blocks away that was also walking distance to Baldwin Market. It was the first home they purchased after renting for years. An interurban electric rail line offered easy access to McAlester from Haileyville and its sister city Hartshorne, only a few miles away. The rail line looped north past Dow Lake where a restaurant and dance hall, boat dock, and picnic area attracted people for leisure time year round.

Upon Bret's return from naval service, he lived with his parents and two young brothers, dutifully completing high school. It was embarrassing being three years older than his classmates were, but he was determined to prepare for college. He reunited with Mrs. Wilson, though both Becky and Robert were off at college. He was developing a passion for opera and Mrs. Wilson helped him further develop his voice. He joined a church choir that winter despite his secular views. He loved the sound of his solos reflected back from the high ceilings. Italian tenor Enrico Caruso was his idle.

Singing was a deeply personal pursuit. The instrument of his voice was his alone to test and develop as far as he could take it. Whenever his tone and pitch were not quite right, he would double down and commit to practice more. What better way to honor life than to seek perfection in the use of your vocal chords? It was right there before him, obvious in its need to be mastered.

Toward the edge of town was a pasture with a few horses, one of which had given birth shortly before Bret's arrival back home. He asked the owner if he could spend time with the foal and help get her started with training. Spending time with the young horse was one of his favorite pastimes and he took a slow and gentle approach to befriending and teaching the intelligent creature.

One day after classes as he walked out toward the sidewalk, Bret passed a group of four boys in their junior year talking. He was not eavesdropping but he caught something that made him slow his pace.

"...there by the janitor's closet. Everyone knows the basement is haunted."

He stopped and approached them. "What is this now?"

"Oh, Hi Bret. I was telling them about this place being haunted. The stories go way back," one of the boys told him.

"Like what?" asked Bret.

"Strange noises. People seeing shadows moving in their peripheral vision. Things like that." They all paused for a moment, then the boy asked Bret, "You believe it?"

"No. I really do not. If you can't prove it scientifically, it is not true. I am going to college to study science. I will come back and tell you if I learn anything about ghosts. But don't count on it," he quipped. "The world is full of real wonders that you can learn all about. Why spend time in idle gossip about things that are not real?" And with that, he set off to walk home wondering the whole way why these stories persisted and hoping his words gave the younger boys some inspiration about how to spend their time.

During that senior year, he took admissions tests and enrolled at Eastern Oklahoma State College. Since his parents could walk to work, they let him borrow their car to drive the thirty miles to classes in Wilburton. He focused on getting through core requirements in preparation for transferring to Oklahoma Agricultural & Mechanical (A&M) College after earning his associate's degree. His favorite classes were in the sciences. Living at home saved him money and allowed him to bicycle on weekends to a filling station in Hartshorne where he worked pumping gas.

He wrote to Sarah and told her how happy he was to be in college. He described his classes and asked how she was doing.

October 14, 1946

Dear Bret,

I am writing with the most exciting news! I am getting married! I have been dating a great fella for almost two years and he finally asked me to marry him. Sam works full time at the paper mill in Kaukauna. He makes a good living and has already applied for a bank mortgage for us to buy a house up there.

There is a lot to do to plan the wedding. Sam's mother, my mother, and I spend our spare time working on invitation lists, decorations, talking to caterers. You may think it sounds like a terrible chore, but I am having the time of my life.

You will be getting an invitation even though I know you cannot really make it so far away and with school and all. But I wish you could. You have been such a good friend. Maybe someday you can come and visit us up here in the north.

Keep me posted on college life.

Best wishes,

Sarah

Bret read this letter with a sinking heart. Certainly, Sarah was not his girlfriend, but he always wondered if she could be someday. Now it was too late. When he received the wedding invitation, he went to the five and dime store and found a nice wedding card. He wrote a brief note inside and addressed it to Mr. and Mrs. Wyckowski.

There were a few girls at school that attracted his attention. Once he invited a girl named Opal to have lunch with him after their morning class. They ate at the school cafeteria and talked about their classes. But the next time he asked if they could have lunch together again, she said she had plans. After he ate his sack lunch in the cafeteria, he went outside and saw her sitting with another boy. They were laughing loudly and he figured he should move on to other prospects. Later in the term, he asked a girl named Hazel out to see a movie. They had a good time and went out a few more times but there did not seem to be any sparks.

The next summer he found a full-time job in Hartshorne waiting tables at a diner. There he met a girl named Clarice, who worked in the back prepping, stocking supplies, and washing dishes. Her round figure and rosy cheeks set off her pleasant demeanor. She wore her blonde hair short and red lipstick. Bret asked her out for a root beer float after work one day. Then they started spending time together here and there. Clarice had an easy nature and was always looking for a reason to be jolly. She talked him into square dancing lessons at the Dow grange hall. Once they got the hang of it, they became regulars at the Saturday evening square dance there. It was hard on Bret's ankle, but he enjoyed it nonetheless.

They would sometimes meet in town for a cup of coffee. It was nice to have someone, a friend who seemed to be available when he was a bit lonely. He thought she seemed down to earth without any notions of things beyond a simple, wholesome life. When she was not working at the diner, she was helping her mother at home or babysitting for her cousins.

Between work and spending time with Clarice, Bret still had idle hours to fill, so he pursued saddle making. He found an old-timer named Henry Crenshaw who had been a saddle maker in his younger days. He walked Bret through the entire thing, starting with making the saddletree out of local beech wood. Eddie went into McAlester with Bret one Saturday to buy tanned cowhide for cutting out the flaps, girth strap, stirrups, and seat. He soaked the seat leather before stretching it tight over the tree, then borrowed leather stamps and punches from Mr. Crenshaw to tool the designs. The finished saddle was beautiful and would became a prized possession.

When the holidays rolled around, Bret received a Christmas card from Sarah announcing the birth of their daughter,

Evelyn, nicknamed Evie. He was genuinely happy for her and replied with a Happy New Year card and a brief note about his life on campus and at the diner, where he still worked on weekends after classes started. He did not mention Clarice. This gave him pause. Since he spent quite a bit of time with her and she was the only person he considered a friend in Oklahoma, why would he not mention her. This gave him a bit of a guilty feeling that he could not pin down inside himself.

Then one day, while they were out for a walk on a warm spring day, Clarice pushed him to make some kind of declaration.

"Bret, I asked you to come for a walk because I want to talk with you about something," she started.

"Okay, what is on your mind?" he replied.

She hesitated then cleared her throat. "Well, there is a boy in town who has walked me home a few times. Yesterday, he asked me out to the movies this Saturday. I told him I would think about it."

"That's nice. Don't worry about the square dance. We do that all the time," he replied.

"So, it doesn't bother you if I date him? Because I sort of thought we were dating. Aren't we dating?" she asked, exasperated.

Bret took a moment to gather his words. "Clarice, I enjoy our time together, but I am not ready to get serious."

"Oh," she said sounding disappointed. "I appreciate your honesty. I think I will accept his movie invitation. And maybe you and I should stop seeing each other."

That gave Bret a moment of pause. "Gosh, have I hurt your feelings. I am sorry if I did. We have a good time together and I just thought we were mostly friends."

"Well, we are now. I will see you around, Bret." With that, she quickened her pace and started in a different direction. Bret stopped and watched her go and wondered if he had been doing something wrong, leading her on. He did not think he had. But then again it sure looked that way.

His thoughts often returned to Sarah and he wondered if he should have been more assertive about his feelings toward her from the beginning. After that, he stayed focused on his studies. He wanted to get his education behind him and establish his career before thinking of starting a family. He definitely wanted a family someday, but his father would tell him that you need to organize your life so the sequence of events makes sense. First things first.

He transferred to Oklahoma A&M in 1948. His parents saw him off on a bus to Stillwater and he lived in a dormitory on campus. He took the bus back home to visit for Thanksgiving and Christmas. During these college years, Bret was quickly losing his hair. Premature baldness seemed to run in the men of his family and there was nothing to do about it. He resigned himself to his ever-shrinking hairline, but grew a beard worn in a goatee to make up for it.

In Stillwater, he found a voice coach in the music department and continued working on perfecting his vocal acuity. The coach taught classical opera and Bret quickly excelled. It was hard to practice in the dorm without a ribbing from the other students, so he would walk out into the football field to practice. One of the things he enjoyed about Stillwater was the churches. He started attending random churches to fill his Sundays and asked the pastors if he might sing during the services. He became a regular guest soloist at several of the churches, his voice reverberating through the expansive spaces.

During his junior year, he received a letter from Sarah announcing the birth of her second child, Jenny. Due to his late graduation from High School, Bret was now twenty-five years old and feeling like time was slipping by too quickly. In addition to school, he needed to start getting some practical experience in his field. Between his baccalaureate graduation and the start of graduate school, he took a temporary nine-month job in Florida with the US Fish and Wildlife Service. His goal was eventually to find permanent employment with that agency or a similar state agency.

His year in Florida reminded him of being in the south pacific. It was warm and humid and everyone seemed a bit more relaxed. Florida was under development and the influx of people was affecting the wild freshwater fish populations. The hatchery was set up to closely monitor the situation and boost species that were waning. While he was there, he dated the hatchery secretary, Kate Lusk. She was recently divorced and had two little girls. He really liked her and found her attractive in a way Clarice never was. She was smart and driven to succeed on her own. She was not looking for a husband, which added to her allure.

In fact, she had a rule about never having a second date with a man. She accepted dinner dates and dancing dates and walks on the beach dates because she wanted adult companionship. But she was terrified to get into a relationship. Her first marriage ended badly and she did not want to repeat that heartache ever again. However, she and Bret just sort of fell together having proximity to each other. They did not have money for much more than walks on the beach or day picnics out hiking with her kids. The casualness of their outings made them less worrisome for Kate.

Bret's father taught him never to make love to a woman until he was married to her, but now he wondered if the rule held true with a divorcee with two children. He found her very attractive and the more time they spent together, the more relaxed and natural they were with each other. He felt he saw her for who she truly was, with bare feet on the beach and sand in her hair. It seemed inevitable when they finally slept together after an evening at her beach cottage. He was smitten.

She, however, shrank back into her shell, acting as though something terrible had happened. He gave her some space and then tried to talk to her about her obvious distress. Finally, she talked it out with him.

"I am so sorry, Bret. You are a wonderful man and you did nothing wrong. I just made a commitment to work on my independence and caring for my children. I really do not want to be distracted from that path," she told him.

"Okay. I understand," he said, unconvincingly. "I really like our time together and you are the best thing that has happened to me. I thought you felt the same way."

She gathered her thoughts carefully. "Bret, I hope we can spend a lot of time having fun before you leave to go back to school. But let's not lose sight of our goals as individuals."

When it was time to return to Stillwater, Bret was deeply conflicted. He did not want to leave her. He proposed that he discontinue his studies for a while and stay on in Florida. But she talked him out of it. She really liked him but thought it was reckless for him to abandon his career path. In the end, they parted ways, promising to write to each other. It was like his relationship with Sarah all over again, but maybe a little more bitter after their shared intimacy.

Bucksport

MAINE, 1890: NELL CHANDLER had no intention of spending the afternoon sitting in a sewing circle. She told her mother that was where she was going so she could have some time alone to think. She was walking along the edge of the high water line, stepping from rock to rock. The tide was on its way out now. She could see the fort across the river and the ferry coming back across. The sky was leaden and could rain on her at any time, but she did not care.

The other girls in the sewing circle were her friends, but her very best friend was Emily Jenkins. Emily had thick curly brown hair and huge brown eyes, in contrast to Nell's pale skin, eyes and straight hair. She also had a lovely singing voice. They had been best friends since first grade. At fifteen, the girls were keen to attract suitors and spent much time discussing the subject. But they both felt that the available single young men were all a little boring. They both wanted some excitement in their lives. Emily had gone to Bangor with her parents for the weekend where she would be fitted for two new dresses for the summer season.

The fabric, ordered ahead and delivered on the train from Boston, had arrived two weeks earlier.

The sewing circle was working on items for their trousseaus. Emily's project was an ambitious one, a wedding ring quilt in pinks and greens. Other girls were working on table linens and finely embroidered bed linens. Nell was having a hard time getting started. Last week she just helped Emily with her project. She thought it would be easier to get started on something if she could actually envision herself married.

She watched her mother and thought life as a wife looked tedious. Her mother cooked, cleaned, washed clothes, did the shopping, and tried to please her husband. Nell's father was the postmaster. He made a good living, but he did not really seem to enjoy it. After work, he went to the tavern with most of the other men in town. Emily's parents ran the tavern where they served beer brought by wagon from Brewer, which was upriver across from Bangor. With Emily's family in Bangor overnight, the tavern would be closed, so her father would be home early today.

She walked for an hour and then made her way back up the steep hill to their house on Elm Street. Her mother was finishing the evening meal, which was clam chowder and bread from the bakery. She looked up when Nell came in and asked her to set the table.

"How was the sewing circle today?" her mother asked.

"I didn't go, Mum," she said, hanging her coat on a hook in the hall.

"Then where have you been all afternoon?" her mother looked up concerned.

"Just out walking. I have not started a project of my own yet and Emily is in Bangor with her parents," Nell said sullenly.

"Well, maybe I can help you get something started. How about a crochet project? That can be very relaxing once you get the rhythm of it," her mother said encouragingly. "Can you get the butter out of the larder, please?"

"Maybe," Nell said absently, related to the crochet idea, as she retrieved the butter.

Her mother let the silence hang between them for a moment. "You seem out of sorts, dear."

Nell sighed slowly. "Since I finished school, there is nothing to focus on. I can help you with household chores, or go to the sewing circle, or go for a walk. It is not very inspiring."

"It's your age. You are naturally restless. Perhaps you and I should take the buggy to Bangor sometime and look around. We could pick out some fabric for a project for you there. They have more of a selection," her mother offered.

"That would be nice, Mum," she replied without enthusiasm.

Her father came through the door, taking off his hat and coat in the hallway.

"Hello, dear," her mother said and kissed him lightly on the cheek.

"Hello. The tavern was closed today, so I am home early."

"Yes, I see that. And anticipated it. Supper is all ready," her mother said.

"Well, that is fine," he said sitting down at the table. "My noon dinner seems a long time ago."

Maynard Chandler was a small man with dark hair and mustache that he turned up at the corners. Geneva, his wife of sixteen years, was small and fair, like their only child Nell. They married when Geneva turned seventeen. Maynard was five years older. Geneva grew up on a dairy farm just outside of town and Maynard was the son of a fisherman. They both completed school through the eighth grade.

"Nell and I were thinking about making a trip up to Bangor sometime soon to do some shopping," Geneva told her husband.

"What day?" Maynard asked.

"Doesn't really matter. Maybe Saturday?" Geneva replied setting down a bowl of chowder in front of him.

"Alright," he replied as he buttered a thick piece of brown bread. "I will have the horse hitched to the buggy and ready by 8:00 in the morning."

"Sounds good," Geneva said and smiled first at him, and then at Nell, who did not reciprocate.

After they all ate a few bites, Maynard said, "I met someone new today. A man named Atkins here from Vermont. Says he is planning on starting up a fish hatchery out on Craig Brook, there by Alamoosook."

"A fish hatchery? Why? The ocean has plenty of fish to feed everyone," Geneva replied.

"The fish won't be to eat. Says they are for restocking the rivers to build up the salmon population. He went to college to study conservation. He learned that the dams on the rivers are depleting the species because they can't go upstream to spawn and lay their eggs," Maynard reported.

"That sounds like a big undertaking. How is he paying for it?" asked Geneva.

"Says he is talking to the federal government about partnering with him," Maynard said.

Nell half heard all this without interest. She was thinking about the trip to Bangor and what she would wear. If she wanted to wear her dark blue bonnet, she needed to mend the hem on her blue dress. Finally, something to focus on.

The journey would take about three and half hours with their horse, Prancy. She was a spirited mare with a fast pace, that is if you could keep her down to a walk. She loved going off on an adventure. They would have three hours in town and be back by 6:00 in the evening at the latest.

The trip to Bangor was mostly uneventful. It was a mild autumn day, with the sun filtered through high clouds. They greeted people they met on the road, most of which they knew or recognized. Just beyond Orrington they passed a funeral in progress. The hearse wagon pulled by two black horses waited by the road, while the small group stood by the open grave. The minister could be heard speaking softly. Geneva slowed Prancy down to a slow walk as they passed.

"Poor souls, mourning the departed," Geneva said quietly.

Nell stared at the people, wondering who had died. She said a quick private prayer for them all, the living and the dead.

When they crossed the bridge into Bangor, they left the horse and buggy with a livery stable on Franklin Street and walked through the bustling downtown.

They went to Chapman's Clothing Company to see the latest styles, then to the dry goods store to see what fabric was in stock. Nell chose coordinating gray and sage green prints. Her mother always told her these colors accentuated her gray/green eyes. They walked through Haymarket Square and picked up fresh produce, then had noon dinner at a small Irish pub serving corned beef and cabbage.

On the way home in the late afternoon, they once again passed the graveyard and saw the mound of fresh dirt over the new grave. It sent a shiver up Nell's spine to think of being buried under the ground.

O N MONDAY OF THE next week, Nell and Emily walked north out of town to look for rosehips and autumn olives. Swinging a basket on her arm, Emily chatted away about gossip from the tavern. She spent most of her time there, helping her parents.

"Everyone is talking about a newcomer starting a fish hatchery," Emily said.

"I heard about him from my father. He is planning to settle on Craig Brook," Nell said.

"Well, until he builds a place to stay out there, he is at the Inn," Emily reported. "I caught a glimpse of him. He is fairly young, maybe just out of college."

"Is he good-looking?" Nell asked.

"Don't know. I have not seen him up close. But I figure he will be in the tavern eventually," Emily speculated. "Unless he doesn't drink."

"Not many people around here who don't drink," Nell said. "At least men. There are plenty of women who don't."

"And plenty who do," Emily said. "Sometimes they come into the tavern with their husbands, but never alone. I suspect a lot of women drink in private in their homes."

"I can't imagine my Mum drinking. She is much too proper," Nell said.

"My Mum has a drink after the tavern closes almost every night. Says it helps her sleep," Emily said. "She offers me a little beer sometimes."

"Do you like it?" Nell asked.

"It's not bad, but I can't imagine drinking it every day like the men who come in," Emily said.

They found olives to gather and took them home to Geneva who was always looking for fresh ingredients. Emily's mother, on the other hand, only cooked the items served at the tavern, which included fried clams, egg salad sandwiches, and fish stew. If her husband or daughter wanted anything else, she sent them to the restaurant at the Inn.

Jed Prouty Inn was a stately two-story structure with a wide front porch facing the river. It was the only lodging available for travelers or newcomers. The restaurant on the first floor served a variety of fare prepared from local ingredients. Beef, pork, and chicken were usually available from the butcher shop, but they also prepared fresh game brought in by the hunters.

The Innkeeper's wife prepared desserts. They also stocked a larger selection of alcohol than the local tavern, including whiskey, brandy, and wine. Ship captains and merchants sat near the large fireplace in the lobby sipping drinks in the evening, whereas the laymen patronized the tavern down on the next block.

The following day Nell stopped by the tavern to see if Emily could get away to walk to the bakery shop with her. They set off arm in arm, deep in conversation, down the sidewalk. When they turned the corner, they collided with a man in a tall hat and stylish coat. They all began apologizing at once and then they all started laughing.

He was tall and very handsome and both girls blushed at their own thoughts.

"I am so very sorry, ladies. Please allow me to introduce myself. I am Charles Atkins," and he bowed chivalrously. "May I ask who I have just nearly run over in my haste?"

"Nell Chandler," she said smiling and curtsied following his lead.

"Miss Emily Jenkins," and she curtsied as well, feeling foolish but enjoying the levity.

"Glad to make your acquaintance. Miss Chandler, you must be the postman's daughter?"

"Yes, sir," Nell said.

"And I have heard the tavern keepers are named Jenkins. Are they your parents?" he asked Emily.

"They are," Emily said.

"Well, now that we are acquainted, I hope to see you both again soon," and he tipped his hat and walked away up the street. The two girls stood staring after him.

"Did you see his eyes?" Emily whispered.

"Stunning," Nell whispered back.

"He is such a gentleman. And so fabulously tall," Emily said.

Nell swallowed hard and slowly turned away as did Emily. They locked arms once again and walked on slowly, both deep in thought.

When they arrived at the bakery the smell of fresh-baked bread made their mouths water. Nell bought a loaf of rye bread and half a dozen yeast rolls to have with dinner. Geneva baked their bread often but she had to admit that the town bakery had a superior product. The rolls were extra fluffy and the loaves of bread had the best buttery crust. Sometimes it was worth the extra cost.

On the way back, Nell ducked into the tavern with Emily and took a stool at the end of the bar. Emily went behind the bar with Hannah and put on an apron.

"Good day, Nell. How is your mother getting on?" Hannah asked.

"She is fine. Although I can't understand how she can go day in day out being cooped up in the house," Nell said. "I have to get out for some fresh air every day."

"Me, too. Sometimes I just walk around the block to hear the birds singing and breathe fresh air. That bread smells glorious!" Hannah said, sticking her face into the paper wrapper and taking a long deep breath.

The dim bar was mostly empty, except for Paul Withers sitting half way down the bar. He turned his head and tipped his hat to Nell who looked away immediately. Since graduating from school, she felt like she was on display for all the single men in town. Paul was probably thirty years old and smelled like fish. She did not want to encourage him in any way. Hannah saw this interaction and winked at Nell. She understood all too well from Emily about how the girls were feeling these days. Nell and Emily discussed everything and Emily in turn shared everything with her mother.

After Paul paid and left the bar, Hannah leaned on the counter and gave Nell a knowing look. Then she began reminiscing about how she met Peter. Emily had heard it all before and busied herself tidying up and sweeping the floor.

"Peter was such a handsome young man when we met. My goodness, I could hardly think of anything else. My father worked at the dry goods store and sometimes I would go there to visit him during the day. One day Peter came in with his older brother to buy nails for the barn they were building. Peter kept catching me staring at him. I had seen him around before, but something was different that day. He suddenly seemed more like a man and less like a boy. I wondered if he was thinking the same sort of thing about me.

"After that, I kept a look out for him around town and found ways for us to encounter each other, seemingly by accident. I spent a lot of time thinking up things I could say to him. Then I would forget what they were when he was standing in front of me. When I think back about how shy and silly I was, it's a wonder he ever asked me for a date. While I was acting like a fool, any other girl in town could have attracted his attention. There's a lesson in all this, girls. Don't expect love to find you. You need to know it when you see it and take matters into your own hands," she said wistfully, staring out the small north-facing window. "You have to make your own luck in this world."

Nell was listening closely, and thinking about Mr. Atkins. He was the most interesting person that had come through town that she could remember. She secretly vowed that she would not be shy around him, but try to be witty and charming next time they met.

She bid Hannah and Emily goodbye and walked home with the fresh bread, all the while wondering what was in store for her. Would she live in this small town all her life? Would she marry a man that drank at the tavern every night while she kept his supper warm for him? She hoped there was something more for her. She wanted adventure, excitement, and love.

The wind picked up turning her nose red by the time she got home. Her mother was sitting at the kitchen table writing a list of some sort. Nell put the bread in the larder and poured a basin of warm water from the kettle. She took it to her room and washed her hands and face in front of the mirror. She looked closely at her features, examining her small mouth, pointed chin, rosy cheeks and windblown hair. She looked younger than she felt and wondered when she could successfully declare herself grownup.

Each evening after supper, she sat with her parents in the front room facing the street. Her mother usually was sewing or mending something. Her father read the newspaper, reporting to the family on items of interest, and told stories about things he had heard that day at the post office or the tavern. He knew everyone in town and gathered bits of gossip into stories.

"Mrs. Mather told me today that she believes there is a thief in our midst. Two of her chickens went missing and then the milk can was taken right off her front porch. I told her that maybe dogs got her chickens and the wind blew her empty milk can down the street. But then Mr. Hanson said that he saw tracks in his backyard that were neither his nor his wife's. So, maybe there is mischief about. Who would walk through someone else's back yard?" he wondered.

"Maybe it was Mrs. Mather looking for her chickens and milk can," offered Geneva.

"In any event, Gracen Conner mailed a package today to his brother in Augusta. It was rather large and made me wonder what was inside," Maynard said. "After he left I noticed that whatever was inside was starting to poke out the side. So I had to open it up so I could repackage it properly, you know. It was a good-sized sharp knife. Now why would he send something like that? Surely there are stores in Augusta to buy such things. It made me wonder if it might not rightfully be his and he was trying to pass it off to someone out of town."

"Are you accusing Gracen Conner of stealing, Maynard? You cannot possibly know what the story is behind the knife," his wife admonished.

"No. No, I cannot. But it does make one wonder," he said wistfully.

This kind of conversation occurred every evening. Nell half listened and half day dreamed. She kept trying to imagine herself sitting in a parlor listening to her husband tell tales of his day. How much would you have to love a man to find this interesting and comfortable - safe and sound in a solid marriage and bored to tears? The thought of it made her want to scream.

She decided that she would need to dream up some adventure for Emily and her for the next day. Anything out of the ordinary would do. Maybe they should go spy on Mr.

Atkins at the Inn. Surely, they could think up some excuse to run into him again. They also needed to make sure he did not get bored and leave town. Maybe they could provide him with a mystery to solve like in the magazines. They could leave him notes that he would have to decipher to find out who wrote them. This idea filled her head with ideas of messages to leave in mysterious notes and she absent mindedly drifted off toward her room to get ready for bed, forgetting to say goodnight to her parents.

Solace

As soon as Bret returned to Oklahoma, his graduate studies began. He once again stayed in the dormitory to save money, but this time he had a room to himself. He made his bed every morning just as he had since he was a child. The top of his dresser and desk, as well as much of the floor, were littered with books, notebooks, and study materials. He had a large window overlooking the campus lawn. He was focused on wildlife biology and deep in his study and research routine when he received a letter from Sarah.

November 5, 1950
Dear Bret,

I have sad news that I can barely bear to write. Sam died in an accident at the mill in August. It was horrible the way he died and the only solace I have is that he died quickly. The company that owns the mill made me sign papers stating that I would not sue them for liable. How could I know if there was any wrongdoing on their part? No one saw it happen. But it did feel very insensitive that they asked me to sign the papers.

I sold the house because I have no way to pay the mortgage. I moved back in with my parents. I spend a lot of time just sitting and staring out the window. I have not worked since I got married and don't know where to begin. I have two toddlers to care for, but I am grateful for them. Otherwise, I don't think I could get out of bed in the morning.

It tears me apart to think that Sam will not be able to see his children grow up. It honestly makes me hope ghosts do exist and he can somehow be close to them from the hereafter. I think I should encourage them to have an open mind about it when they are older.

I would really appreciate hearing from you. All my high school friends are happily married and I don't feel like being around that. I am lost and just need contact beyond my parents.

Sarah

Bret was grief-stricken at the thought of Sarah in pain. He wished he could go to her and put his arms around her but he could not leave school. He sat down that moment and wrote her a letter.

November 10, 1950

Oh my dear Sarah! I am so very sorry to hear about your husband's untimely death. I have always wanted only the best for you and your letters made me happy when I could tell you were happy. Please know you are in my thoughts and I will write often during this time of grief.

You have been such a steady friend over all these years. I miss being able to talk with you in person. If I could afford it I would call you on the telephone, but long distance calls are so expensive. I do not even call my parents, but write to them instead.

To save money I started a new plan of only eating twice a day in the late morning and early evening. This works out okay because I do not have any spare time for exercise that would require more nutrition. I am looking forward to starting my career and having a regular income to depend on. I also want to be able to come see you.

I spend all my time in the biology lab, the library or my dorm room, which tends to be a big mess. I have a lot less leisure time now that I am in graduate school, especially because my advisor's office is right across the hall from the lab. He would know if I was slacking on my work. I also serve as the lab aid, so when students are not keeping up, I spend time helping them along.

I will write again later this week, so you have another letter to look forward to. Try to keep your spirits up and be strong.

I miss you,
Bret

He put it in the mail an hour later, all the while thinking of other things he might have written. When he got home, he jotted notes to help him write the next one. He had never lost someone close to him. He could hardly imagine losing a spouse. He thought about his parents and wondered how one survives the other after living with their lives so deeply entangled for many years. But mostly he thought of Sarah and her grief, and about her children losing their father.

Later that week he wrote again.

November 15, 1950
Dearest Sarah,
You have been on my mind constantly. I cannot imagine the grief you are feeling. Please know you are in my thoughts. As a scientist, I do not take much stock in prayers, but I have been trying. If there is a God I want to make sure he knows about you and sends you comfort. And if there is no God, I am sending you all the comfort I can muster.

Life is a mystery. I often wonder what we are doing here, but there is no answer. We just have to keep on. My parents told me at an early age that my spiritual beliefs were my own. They would never impose any belief on me, and told me never to let anyone else do it either. It is personal and private and we each have to take that journey in our own heads.

Nevertheless, I have spent a fair amount of time in church these past few years. I have practiced using my voice to sing since I was young, but singing in a church is the best. The acoustics create a sound different from any other. I found a used record player at a junk shop and an old Caruso recording. I work hard to raise my voice to his level of perfection.
Keep your chin up,
Bret

The next day he received a letter from Sarah that the floor monitor had put under his door.

December 13, 1950

Dear Bret,

I just received your letter. It was so good to hear from you. I cannot tell you how much it meant to me to see that you wrote right away.

My little ones need me so much and are not old enough to understand their father is gone. They keep asking about him. It pains me to try to explain death to them. I wish they did not need to know. I say he is in heaven, but that means nothing to them.

Today I washed my hair, put on a dress and lipstick and bravely went out to the store for groceries for my mother. She has been trying to get me to go out without her and this was the first time. Then I saw a friend with her arm through her husband's walking toward me down the sidewalk and I ducked into a hardware store so they would not see me. I cannot talk to anyone and I especially cannot hear words of sympathy without crying.

The clerk at the hardware store swooped down on me immediately and I had to pretend I needed a hammer. After he showed me the merits of all the hammer styles, I said thank you and left the store. I am sure he thinks I am crazy.

Then I went home without any groceries. But my mother already knows I am crazy these days, so she was not surprised.

Write back soon,
Sarah

The story about the hardware store became a standing joke between them. She made up stories about her shopping trips to more unlikely places and he in turn made suggestions for her next outings. These included the paint store where he suggested she spend a whole afternoon choosing colors and finishes for an imaginary house she will live in one day. She told him she went to a sewing machine shop and asked the clerk to demonstrate the merits of all their high-end machines, then asked if they could teach her how to sew. He said she should go to the train station and ask the ticket clerk to help her plan a trip around the country to visit all the national parks. She said she was going to the appliance store to look at washing machines and ask them to teach her how to do laundry successfully. She went to buy fabric for her mother to make new kitchen curtains but forgot to convert the inches into yards and came home with a whole bolt of fabric. Since it was not returnable and so as not to be wasteful, she was making six matching red-checked dresses for herself. Her stories became more and more outlandish and though written with deadpan facetiousness, they made Bret laugh aloud.

He in turn tried to make her laugh with his own wildly made-up stories about lab accidents. He said that he was making slides of various yeasts when he took a break for lunch. It was a very warm day and when he returned to the lab, the yeast had started to grow and ooze out over the open window onto pedestrians below. He told her that the president of the college came by to see his research and he had to hide in the closet because he had just spilled acid on his pants and taken them off. After dark, he ran back to his dorm building under cover of night with no pants on.

The letter writing became addictive for both of them and it was unusual to receive only one letter in the course of a week. As their correspondence continued, their fondness for each other grew. Bret's salutations turned to "My lovely Sarah" and "My funny girl," and he closed with things such as "thinking of you with loving thoughts" and "your knight in shining armor." Sarah followed suit, starting with "my dear friend" and ended with "love, Sarah."

When Bret went to see his parents during spring break in March 1951, he talked to them about her. Elsie was at the stove in the kitchen but could see and hear the conversation in the front room.

"Hey Dad, do you remember Mrs. Barker's daughter Sarah that used to come over to camp sometimes?" he asked.

"Yes, son. Lovely girl."

"Well we have stayed in touch over all these years. Her husband died last year in an accident at the mill."

Elsie looked up from her stirring. "I am sorry to hear that. How horrible."

"I know. It really is." Bret said. "We started writing a lot after she told me. She said she really needed the support of a friend, but I think it has turned into something more than that."

"That is wonderful, son." Eddie said. "Do you think you two will get together?"

"There is quite a distance to overcome, but I was thinking of paying her a visit. Maybe taking the train up there sometime this summer."

"Sounds like a good idea," and his father smiled warmly. "If I teach up there again this summer you could ride with me then take the train back."

"Great! That would be a fun road trip," Bret said.

Just then, his two younger brothers raced in, one with a skinned knee that was bleeding and all attention turned to them. They did not talk about it again on that visit, but wrote back and forth making plans. Toward the end of June, Eddie, with Bret's brothers now ages twelve and fifteen, picked Bret up in Stillwater. They drove to Wisconsin in three days, camping along the way. It was one of the best times for all of them.

Bret had started writing to Sarah in early April about possibly coming to visit, and kept her posted on the developing plans. When he arrived, she was sitting on the front porch in a pink and white sleeveless dress drinking lemonade waiting for him. She had grown into such a beautiful woman. They embraced, unloaded his suitcase, and Eddie and the boys set off for the camp. Sarah led Bret in the house by the hand where her parents greeted him warmly. The children were playing with the neighbor kids in the backyard, but soon entered the house noisily to meet the guest. Four-year-old Evie had blonde shoulder-length curls and bright blue eyes. Two-year-old Jenny had short red hair, brown eyes, and a splattering of freckles across her nose.

Bret stayed in the spare room for four nights, while the young couple spent time together. They went on picnics with the children, swam in the lake, ate ice cream cones, and visited with her parents in the evening after the kids were in bed.

One day when the two of them sat alone on the front porch together, Bret said, "I have been thinking a lot about the grief you were left with when Sam died. I admit I have not yet had to suffer a loss of that kind, but I grew up learning that keeping busy is the best way to manage your own thoughts. Sometimes too much time on your hands can foster unwanted thoughts and sadness."

"Yes, I can agree with that. But sometimes sadness makes it hard to do anything."

Bret thought about that for a moment. He did not want to push her into thinking about unhappiness. He was trying to do the opposite.

"What I mean to say is that I think we all have to keep moving forward, especially when it feels like the world is standing still. Time does not stand still. So, we owe it to ourselves and the people around us to persevere," he said.

They sat in silence for a moment and he began to worry he had said the wrong thing.

"I just want you to know how wonderful you are, Sarah. And if there is ever anything I can do to make you happy, I am right there."

When they said goodnight to each other, they kissed quickly on the cheek in the hallway between them. It was the kiss of a friend. But when it was time to get on the train back to Stillwater, something overcame them both at the thought of parting. They shared a long romantic kiss. Then another. Then one more. The train was already rolling when he finally stepped on.

On the trip back to Stillwater, Bret wrote to her. First, he told her how much he enjoyed their time together and adored her children. He would be ready to defend his thesis at the end of the fall term and planned to apply for a temporary position at Norfork National Fish Hatchery in Mountain

Home, Arkansas. If he got the job, he would move there in January. Then he finally got to his point.

"I do not want to live without you. Will you consider marrying me?"

He received a card in the mail the next week with an illustration of a rainbow trout on the front. Inside was just one word.

YES!

The news delighted Sarah's parents. As the couple wrote back and forth making plans, Sarah's parents decided to give them their 1941 Dodge Town Sedan as a wedding present. Sarah would drive her and the girls down to Arkansas if he got the job, or wherever else if that did not work out. They would be married as soon as they reunited around Christmas time.

Their letters were flying back and forth so fast now that their respective postmen started making jokes to them about their whirlwind romance. Bret applied for the job and worked hard to finish his thesis, which he defended the first week in December. The very next day he received news that he had won the position in Arkansas, and was expected to arrive to begin his duties the second week in January. With time to spare and the weather cooperating, Sarah drove to Haileyville where she and Bret were married in the living room of the Justice of the Peace with his parents, brothers, Aunt Olga, Uncle Ben, Evie and Jenny as witnesses. They all went to dinner at Pete's Place Italian Restaurant in Krebs to celebrate. The waiters served heaps of spaghetti, ravioli, meatballs, sauces, and loaves of bread family style at a long table shared with other patrons, and the whole place shared a toast to the happy newlyweds.

After spending Christmas all together, Bret and his new family bid farewell and drove to Mountain Home, Arkansas to start their new life.

Greener Pastures

THEY RENTED A FURNISHED two-bedroom house in Mountain Home. Sarah worried that Bret's position was only temporary, but Bret insisted it was the road to successful federal employment. He knew it was possible to get into a permanent position by being willing to move for temporary assignments as they came up. He watched the job board at the hatchery office, ever-vigilant for the next opportunity. As it happened, he was able to string together three consecutive temporary assignments in Mountain Home.

Arkansas was green and lush, and poorer than they ever imagined. When Sarah enrolled the girls in school, it was like stepping back in time. The school was a small clapboard structure in need of paint with a wood stove for heat. Though it had plumbing for an indoor toilet, there was no provision for making or serving lunch to the children. The woman who lived next door delivered mashed potatoes and peas each day at noon. On the last day of school before Christmas break, they had slices of thick gingerbread cake as a special treat. Before summer break, they had watermelon. But the rest of the time: mashed potatoes and peas.

Sarah's first instinct was to pack the girls a good lunch, but then she thought of how awkward it would be for them to eat in front of the other children. She counseled them to eat what the other kids did for lunch, and made sure they had a good healthy breakfast and dinner at home.

"If you don't want it, then offer it to someone else," she told them. "But do not say anything bad about the food."

Sarah enjoyed cooking. Her mother had told her to use cookbook recipes but make them better.

"Follow the recipe the first time and then, if it is good, start experimenting to make it better," her mother said. "If it is not good, give up on it and find another recipe. You will learn by doing. The more you cook the better instinct you will have for what makes food better. This goes for everything except baked goods. Breads, cakes, cookies, muffins, or anything like that should only be trifled with by adding, deleting, or substituting fruits and nuts. Or adding more fat to make it richer. The rest of the recipe should be followed as to the ratio of flour, baking powder, baking soda, yeast, salt, etc."

Sarah's mother had a four-year nursing degree, and supplemented that with reading everything she could about nutrition. She counseled Sarah to find ways to incorporate more nutrition into simple recipes. Produce could be cooked down and added to almost any entrée or side dish. She was a big fan of spinach. "No one likes cooked spinach, but the nutritional value is superb. Hide it everywhere in your cooking," she said.

Sarah admired her mother and hoped to become as talented in the kitchen as she was. After cafeteria food all through school, Bret loved everything she made. She had two cookbooks that her mother gave her when she married Sam. The Joy of Cooking and Betty Crocker Cookbook. Sarah did not love any of the recipes found in them, but she liked them well enough to fix them and make them her own. She kept a notebook of her trials and triumphs. It was food-spattered, stained, and dog-eared, but a favorite possession.

Sarah was somewhat appalled to learn that there in the Deep South it was illegal to purchase anything on Sunday related to work, like a broom or a bucket or a hammer. This hit home when she went to the hardware store on a Sunday to purchase a meat grinder for making burger out of beef she had bought in bulk on sale the day before.

"I am sorry ma'am. You can purchase that tomorrow, but I cannot sell it to you today," the clerk told her matter-of-factly. Then pointed to the sign on the wall.

Sarah smiled politely, bid him good day, and walked out rolling her eyes to the heavens.

It all seemed a little backwoods. Making the best of it, they all strove to embrace those woods. Bret wanted to teach the girls all about nature and they spent time hiking, identifying trees, insects, and birds. Sarah was a stay at home Mom and spent all her energy nurturing her children and her marriage. When she was not in the kitchen, she was making the house nice and her family comfortable. It was a challenge to make ends meet between Bret's paychecks, but they did not really need much. The relative poverty of the area did not instill any sense of competition for fashion. It did not matter if they wore the same clothes every week. The government provided Bret with a generous clothing allowance for his uniforms so he ordered the maximum allowed and lived in them. Sarah scouted church bazaars for herself and the girls. They really only needed money for rent, utilities, and food. Occasionally there was a need for new shoes and socks that wore completely out, and car maintenance expenses. Luckily, they were all healthy.

Then Bret decided they needed a television. They were all the rage and Bret would linger in the store looking them over.

Together the couple saved up to buy a Zenith console for Christmas, a huge purchase for them. Thus, they entered the modern age and began the evening tradition of gathering in the front room for broadcast entertainment. In addition to up-to-the-minute news, they watched *The Honeymooner*s, *The Danny Thomas Show*, *Ozzie and Harriet*, *The George Burns and Gracie Allen Show*, and *I Love Lucy*.

They were just one long day's drive from Haileyville and went a few times a year to visit Bret's parents. They all squeezed in making pallets on the floor to sleep. Eddie was passionate about bass fishing and together he and Bret taught the girls about making lures and fishing techniques. Bret's brothers were already well schooled at a young age along with all the Boy Scouts that Eddie nurtured. Elsie and Sarah went to various lakes with them, bringing a picnic and casting out their own lines.

As they sat by the lake, Eddie talked with Bret. "We have been working to save money and want to buy farmland out past the lake in Hartshorne. We are planning to have cows, grow our own hay to winter them over. I have been working with the Ag Extension office of the university to learn the original species of the short grass prairie. It is highly nutritious for livestock."

They fished for a while, then Eddie added, "They have a class on beekeeping and I think we will try it. We could harvest honey and the bees will ensure good cross-pollination of the hay meadow."

"That is great, Dad. How much land are you hoping to get?" Bret asked.

"Well, even though land is less expensive here than most places, it still has a price to negotiate. We will get as much as we can afford. Land is always a good investment," he told his son. "Whatever we buy we can hunt there for deer, duck, and turkeys. Your mother is getting to be a good shot." Elsie overheard them and smiled at her husband.

Both Bret and Sarah wanted to have more children together. Following the counsel of both sets of parents, they decided to wait until Bret found permanent employment. Sarah's mother taught her about using the rhythm method to avoid accidental pregnancy, abstaining during Sarah's ovulation. But in 1955, passion got the better of them after a few New Year's Eve drinks and they conceived. At four months, the pregnancy ended in a miscarriage, which greatly saddened all of them. Sarah explained to the girls and they tried to understand. It opened doors for many conversations about life and death, natural processes, and grief.

The next year, Sarah conceived again. One of Bret's greatest motivations for finding a permanent position was that his family would have health care coverage. As it was, they were concerned about the cost of a hospital stay. Sarah found a midwife and began working with her seven months along to prepare for the birth.

"Are you sure?" Bret asked. "What if there are complications."

"There won't be. Don't you worry. I can do this. I have done it." And she patted his cheek softly with her hand and smiled. "It will be okay."

This plan also gave Evie and Jenny exposure to the miracle of birth. They watched in horrified fascination as their mother's body seemingly turned inside out to deliver them a baby sister. Bret named his first-born child Isabelle.

Evie and Jenny learned to help care for their new baby sister around their schoolwork and playdates with other kids. Bret was intensely interested in their education, believing it was the most important advantage a person could have as imprinted by his parents. He expected top grades from the children, and whenever they brought home anything less, he would say, "You will do better next time." Though he meant only to encourage them, both girls grew to believe it was a mandate.

Isabelle was a happy baby and entertained them all. The sound of the children playing filled their home with a sense of belonging that Bret had little experience with since his two brothers were ten and twelve years younger. Bret was especially smitten with his firstborn and talked of having more children. Bret and Sarah had built their relationship on their shared sense of humor. They enjoyed each other's company and laughed at the antics of their children.

They would sit on the front porch in the evening listening to the frogs singing in the woods, talk about their day.

"I asked at the store today if they had any fresh herbs and you would have thought I was speaking a foreign language. I knew I should have planted a little herb garden. I might need to go into Roanoke sometime soon for a little shopping," Sarah said.

"My math homework is different. I don't know what they want me to do," Evie said.

"Let me look at it with you. We will figure it out together," Bret said and Evie ran to get her papers.

"Today at recess Kevin Ogden peed out of his bellybutton," Jenny reported.

Bret and Sarah busted up laughing much to Jenny's confusion. "He did!" she insisted. "I told him I didn't know how to do that."

Mosquitos started to swarm as the light faded and they moved indoors to work on homework.

"What about your day?" Sarah asked Bret.

"Same old thing. Feeding fish. Cracking jokes with Joe. Tomorrow we need to load a truck for a release into the river," Bret said.

In duty to his growing family, Bret worked hard to seek his next position, realizing there could be no gap in steady employment. One day he came home with a big grin on his face and announced to Sarah that he had been offered a permanent position at a hatchery in Wytheville, Virginia. This permanent classification qualified him for annual raises, health insurance for the family, and a retirement plan. Within a month, they were packed and ready to leave. None of the furniture was theirs, so there was not much. A small trailer hauled all of their household and personal goods. Evie and Jenny cried when they said farewell to best friends.

Nestled in the Blue Ridge Mountains, Wytheville was a tourist destination for those escaping the summer heat at lower elevations. It had the dubious distinction of having had the worst outbreak in the country of polio back in 1950. The town had been put under quarantine. In 1955, the polio vaccine was available and the family was all now vaccinated and undeterred by the town's history. Wytheville had about 5,000 people and was friendly and welcoming.

They moved into a small two-bedroom house on the hatchery grounds. Isabelle's crib was in Bret and Sarah's room, while Evie and Jenny shared the other room. It was a tight fit. They slept on the floor for three nights until they found used beds to buy. Bret found a set of wooden straight-back chairs at a yard sale, which he started sanding to refinish.

He bought a solid wood door at a closeout sale and using his woodworking skills finished it into a dining table, using scrap wood at the hatchery to make legs. After several coats of lacquer, it came out looking as nice as if it was store bought. Once settled, the girls were enrolled in school. In their spare time, they explored the land, finding its treasures in sparkling streams, spring dogwood blossoms, deep deciduous forests, summer berries, and sweeping vistas after a hike to fill their lungs with intoxicating oxygen.

Though they had little cash, they were caught up in the optimism of the 1950s. Young families were growing all around them seeking to heal the insecurities left by the depression and the war years. While in Virginia, Sarah gave birth to a dark haired baby girl. Bret, having named his first-born, left the choice to Sarah. She named the new addition Lydia, after her grandmother.

Virginia was as beautiful as Mountain Home had been. They counted their blessings at living in places where other people spent their hard won vacations. Unfortunately, the house was now far too small and Bret thought he must continue to climb up the ladder of the Fish and Wildlife Service. He saw a position in Pittsford, Vermont. The pay was a bit better, but mostly he applied because he had never seen New England and wanted to embark with his family on another expedition. Vermont was said to be a beautiful place.

Now that Bret had won a non-seasonal position, the government paid for a moving company, even though they had little to move. As soon as they were unpacked at the hatchery house in Vermont, Sarah became pregnant again. When Bret called his parents to tell them the news, they announced they would be making a summer trip to visit. Bret's two younger brothers were now in college and his parents had the freedom to travel.

Bret and Sarah wanted to buy a living room sofa and took this need for a guest bed as an opportunity to buy a foldout sofa bed on credit. This was the very first time they had purchased anything on credit, which was against their principles. Both Bret and Sarah's parents had survived the Great Depression and schooled their children in living on earnings. The only exception would be to buy a house, which was impossible to accomplish without a mortgage.

Elsie and Eddie arrived in the late afternoon. After they greeted all the kids and exclaimed at how much they had grown, Bret took them on a tour of the hatchery. He was especially proud to point out the decorative fish sculptures he had made in his spare time from pieces of strap iron to enhance the place. Sarah made a pot roast with fresh herbs and homemade yeast rolls for dinner.

That evening after all the children were in their beds, Bret's parents sat with the younger couple in the comfort of the living room with the new sofa.

Elsie smiled and told them, "Your grandmother is doing so well for her age. We are pleased to be able to see her anytime at her apartment in McAlester. It's only half a mile from Ben and Olga's house. She is so independent, having groceries delivered rather than asking any of us for help." Bertha had retired at sixty-nine to move near her daughters.

"Ben and Olga are smart," Eddie exclaimed. "They save money and have been investing in mineral rights throughout Pittsburg County. Its likely oil is down there right under our feet. They are also investing in town lots in the up-and-coming town of Crowder north of us on Lake Eufaula."

Eddie turned again and again to talking about the new professional football team in Dallas. The Cowboys were in their second year and Eddie was a huge fan. He told his players at the high school to watch every game they could on television for inspiration.

After more catching up on general news, Eddie took Elsie's hand in his and said, "Son, we have something important we would like to discuss with the two of you. We are concerned about the size of your growing family. It is impractical and frankly a bit irresponsible to keep having children." He spoke kindly while Elsie stared at the floor worrying about her son's feelings. "Five children to feed, clothe and educate is a lot. We feel you and Sarah should think about getting twin beds to help avoid any more pregnancies."

This left Bret and Sarah feeling embarrassed, but they knew his parents only wished the very best for them and the grandchildren. The fifth child was born in Vermont on Thanksgiving Day 1961, and Sarah named her Anne.

Evie and Jenny were now fourteen and twelve years old. The life they had shared for the past seven years was a source of continual conversation between them. They had changed schools every few years, usually in the middle of the school year. It was somewhat of a miracle that they always kept up with their studies and had perfect grades. They had to be nimble and adept at making friends or living without them. The moves were hard for them and made them feel powerless over their own fates.

Meanwhile, their mother kept having babies. This was a point for much consternation. Was Bret making her do it? Did he need all these children to call his own, as if they were not enough? Or was it that he wanted so much to have a son that he would keep trying indefinitely? They scoffed about it and rolled their eyes. Sometimes they thought it made their mother happy, but mostly they thought she agreed to have more children to make Bret happy. But either way, these choices effected all of their lives. More mouths to feed, less to go around, and less attention from their mother.

Bret continued his restless pursuit of advancement. A pay grade increase was available at the hatchery in Cortland, New York, and the family pulled up stakes yet again. They crammed into a small three-bedroom house. The only place for baby Anne's crib was at the end of the hall and the trappings of their lives burdened every inch of space. Sarah enrolled Isabella in Kindergarten even though she would not turn five until after the start of the school year. Three small children were just too much to manage. Though Lydia was mostly potty trained, or housetrained as Sarah called it, she still needed constant monitoring. Sarah started to feel like everything might fall apart, and had nightmares of leaving a child on the bus or forgetting to feed one of them.

Isabella came home from school in tears that she could not explain to her mother. The teacher said she was shy at school and just needed some time to adjust. Anne had a six-week check-up in January, and the pediatrician expressed concern over the alignment of her legs, indicating a slight pigeon toe. A consulting orthopedist confirmed the diagnosis and put full leg casts on the baby for five months. As if it was not enough work to nurse, bathe, and keep a baby in clean diapers now Sarah had plaster casts around which to negotiate.

Then one Saturday the following month, six-year-old Isabella came rushing into the house as Sarah was nursing the baby to report that Lydia was hurt. They heard the crying and found her on the driveway pavement next to the car. Isabella described the scene of Lydia climbing onto the hood in order to jump off, an activity for which she had already been scolded repeatedly. Luckily, nothing was broken but the three-year-old's leg bones were badly bruised requiring a full leg cast to properly heal and avoid further injury. Sarah held it together until she walked through their front door back home and broke down in tears. Bret tried to comfort her with soothing words and gentle compassion, but she wanted to unleash her emotions and break something.

When neighbors moved away in December, they sought to rehome their two cats. Sarah and Bret agreed to take them as a surprise for the children. The story was that Mrs. Claus herself had knocked on the door on Christmas Eve to deliver these special gifts. Whatever their original names may have been, they soon became Grey Fur and Black & White, thus beginning Bret's tradition of bestowing easy to remember pet names based on fur color.

Shortly thereafter, Sarah woke to the sound of trickling water and thought there was a leak somewhere in the house. She followed the sound to the bathroom where she switched on the light to find the extraordinary sight of the black and white cat perched on the toilet seat rim peeing into the bowl. This talent made up for his otherwise indifferent attitude toward his new family. As time went on, they also discovered he knew how to open doors by launching himself, wrapping his front paws around the doorknob, and swinging his body. He also came running when he heard the vacuum cleaner to stretch out on his back and get his belly vacuumed. Never having lived with children, neither cat especially liked petting, much less cuddling. Sarah advised the children to give them a wide berth to avoid scratches requiring the sting of Merthiolate tincture.

As if there was still space, they then adopted a tri-colored beagle mix puppy and named her Rainbow, or Bow for short.

Bret, chasing after a management position, continued to scan all the system-wide openings posted at the hatchery office. Their large family could not comfortably live in such a small house and his income needed improvement to support them all. When an assistant manager position opened in East Orland, Maine in 1963 at Craig Brook National Fish Hatchery, he applied without even consulting Sarah. No need to worry her unnecessarily. If he got the job, it could be their last move for a long time. He waited until the official transfer paperwork came through, then he broke the news. Sarah cried herself to sleep that night as exhaustion and uncertainty overwhelmed her. The older girls were despondent to the announcement they both knew meant saying goodbye to friends and starting at yet another school. Bret hoped with every fiber of his being that he was doing the right thing for his family.

In order to transport everyone, Bret purchased a Chevrolet Greenbrier Bus with three bench seats. The back seats faced each other making it easy for all the kids to interact. This "school bus" embarrassed the older girls to no end, as vans had not yet entered the popularity they would gain in a few years. The trip to Maine was long and often barren as they passed miles and miles of dense evergreen forests. It seemed to Sarah that they must be about to enter Canada by the middle of the second day. They arrived in Bucksport late in the evening and collapsed in two rooms at the Springs Motel, with all the kids, cats and dog piled in. In the morning, they bought groceries and ate in the motel room while they packed up for the last five miles to their new home.

Everyone looked wide-eyed at the town for the first time in daylight. A bridge connected Bucksport to Verona Island and then on over to the far side of the Penobscot River. They could see Fort Knox, built in 1844 to protect against British insurrection from Canada. The air was foul with low tide mud flats and the stench of the paper mill. This made them all look at each other out of concern for what they had gotten themselves into this time. They drove east, crossed the Orland River at the quaint village of Orland and its large historic homes from early in the previous century, which gave them hope things were not too bleak ahead.

Eventually they pulled off the main road at the center of East Orland where a small group of old clapboard houses and a one-room post office bordered a dammed pond. They crossed a narrow bridge under which passed the runoff from the pond spillway. Along the mile-long dirt road to the fish hatchery, they passed a few homes, some no more than shacks in the woods.

Then the view opened onto the shining Alamoosook Lake. They stopped briefly at the hatchery office for Bret to say hello and then went on to their new house. Across a narrow bridge over babbling Craig Brook they entered through brick columns past an enormous oak, elm, and maple tree to a circular drive and large white house with dark green trim. The garage door was unlocked for them and they entered from there into the kitchen. Everyone was speechless wandering the empty house.

The kitchen had suffered updating with yellow and grey linoleum flooring, white metal cabinets, Formica countertops, and reallocation of some of the space for a small half bathroom. In contrast, the rest of the house inspired awe with its Victorian grandeur. Wide hardwood floorboards, solid four-panel doors with glass doorknobs, and large double-hung windows with original wavy glass panes were in every room. A built-in beveled glass china cabinet and bay window looked out onto an old rose garden.

The living room featured large windows facing the lake and a corner fireplace with carved wooden mantle and beveled mirror. Across a central hallway with the main entrance were two additional rooms, both with fireplaces in the wall between them. One of these had an additional outside entry through a mudroom.

Two staircases led to the second floor. One was open to the central front hall and had a beautiful carved banister. The other was narrower and enclosed at the back of the house off the kitchen.

Upstairs a central hall opened onto four bedrooms, a covered balcony with a view of the lake, a bathroom with a cast iron claw-foot tub, a large walk-in linen closet, and access to the attic stairway. Wallpapers, no two the same, wrapped each room in cozy warmth. Alcove nooks in the hall and bedrooms offered cozy intimate spaces. A wide wrap-around screened porch looked out over the sloping lawn toward the lake.

Bret smiled broadly when he saw the look on Sarah's face. After all those years of transfers and small modern ranch houses, this place was magnificent. There was room for all of them, a lake practically in their front yard, and acres of property to explore. The fire lane through the woods off the back yard led to a two-track rustic road over granite steps to the top of Great Pond Mountain.

The magnificent house was built in 1897 for Charles Atkins, a pioneering conservationist who in 1890 had developed the property to preserve the Atlantic salmon population as one of the first federal fish hatcheries. The clear cold glacial Craig Brook water was ideal to feed the fish rearing troughs and raceways. A spring filled the cistern for the house with cold sweet fresh water.

Their meager furnishings, which arrived later that day in the moving van, were lost in the spacious vacuum. Sarah and Bret designated two adjoining bedrooms with fireplaces and wooden mantels to Evie and Jenny. As teenagers, they needed their space and privacy. The younger children would share the nursery, a small blue bedroom at the back of the house. Bret made immediate plans to build bunk beds for Isabelle and Lydia. Anne's crib tucked perfectly into the nursery alcove. The two extra rooms on the first floor, which had once been the hatchery office and receiving room, would become a children's playroom and a sewing room.

Sixty dollars in rent, extracted monthly from Bret's pay, bought him the privilege of raising his family in the enormous house. The Craig Brook Hatchery was noteworthy for its successful conservation work and Bret was proud to be part of it.

He could not wait to tell his father the rich history of the place. Thus began a new chapter in a place vastly different from anywhere they had lived. It would shape them in numerous ways as together they would experience riches of the soul that only love and nature can provide.

And, just like that, time slowed down. They were home. The clouds of uncertainty cleared away and the turmoil faded into the past. All those crazy moves to all those inadequate homes were now just family stories of their early years of marriage.

Downeast

GETTING TO KNOW THEIR new place as spring turned into summer 1963 was a different journey for each of them. Bret started what would be a bit of a rocky path with his new boss. The manager was loud and an abrasive know-it-all of an unusual sort. The program, however, was solid and making substantial progress in its goal of restoring the Atlantic salmon population in the tributaries of the region. The secretary, Cleo, was professional and always well dressed. Bret's primary work mate in the daily duties of the hatchery was of old Maine stock, and a salt of the earth. John did not say much, but when he did, it was usually humorous; at least once Bret got the hang of the deep Maine accent.

For him, being settled down without the burden of looking for the next move, left him free to explore his many interests. They came and went without warning and always surprised Sarah. Whatever current obsession he was embracing, it would fill all of his spare time: after work in the evening and all of the hours of the weekends. The first would involve furnishing for their large home.

Sarah wanted to learn the lay of the land and know her children were safe. While Evie and Jenny, at fourteen and sixteen set off to explore, Sarah took the three little ones with her on daily outings. They walked the shoreline, explored the woods along the fire lane, and visited all the many water hazards in the shape of raceways and holding ponds. At the bottom edge of the front lawn, a pipe protruded vertically from the ground providing a steady stream of water into a shallow pool which then disappeared underground to run down to the lake. The sweet, clear, ice-cold glacial spring water was unrivaled. People who did not have running water brought jugs and filled them at the pipe a few times a week.

The girls were a curiosity for the neighbors. Five girls, all as different as could be. They stood together in front of the mirror trying to find similarities without much success. Evie was tall, with wavy blonde hair, small features, and blue eyes. Sarah said she resembled Sam's mother. Jenny was shorter with auburn hair and brown eyes, and looked like Sarah's mother, complete with freckles. Isabelle's face most resembled Sarah's features. She was tall, had brown hair, but, unlike Sarah, she had blue eyes. Lydia looked like Elsie with dark hair nearly black and hazel eyes. Anne looked like Eddie's mother with strawberry blond hair, green eyes, and freckles. Knowing they all looked like one of their ancestors helped make up for not looking like sisters at all.

Bret came home from work, a short walk from the hatchery office. He stood in the kitchen drinking a beer while Sarah worked on preparing baked lasagna riddled with fresh vegetables, a salad of baby greens with grated carrots and cucumber slices, and warm garlic bread.

"We walked up to Craig Pond for today's outing. I had to carry Anne all the way back," she told him. Just then, Anne crawled out from under the table where she was hiding and eavesdropping, and ran toward the toy room to find her sisters.

Bret knew Sarah was worrying as all mothers do in a new environment. He sought to put her mind at ease. "Sweetheart, this is a safe place to raise children. No poisonous snakes. No tornadoes, hurricanes, or earthquakes," he teased. "And I am always here onsite, usually just a shout away."

"Well, there is a lot of water. Evie and Jenny can swim, but we need to teach the little ones," she replied.

"Of course. As soon as the water in the lake is warm enough. John stuck a thermometer in it today, still below 50 degrees," he reported.

At six o'clock Sarah called the kids to dinner. They all squeezed in around the table Bret made in Virginia. Sarah stood to fill the plates for the young children, and then passed the bowls for everyone else. The sun was warm and intensely bright through the dining room bay window and Sarah decided she would need to make a window covering if they were going to eat there each evening.

Breakfast and lunch were a different matter. On weekdays, Sarah made breakfast for Bret, but everyone else ate whenever they got up that summer. Evie and Jenny made their own cereal and toast. Sarah fed the others when they came peeping like little birds, usually all at once. Bret came home every day for lunch. Sarah always tried to cook enough for dinner so he could have warmed up leftovers for lunch the next day. The older girls made themselves sandwiches when they wanted, and once again, the little ones came to her when they were hungry for lunch. There did not seem to be any reason for a schedule until the school year started.

The manager and John told Bret about a path through the woods to a good swimming place for children. One evening they all walked down the fire lane, found the trailhead, which was barely discernable then, and followed it to the water's edge.

There was a little gravelly beach and a rock protruding out of the water about 20 feet from shore. The space in between was shallow. On the other side, the ground fell away for diving in to. It was, in fact, a great place for swimming lessons, which began later that summer.

Isabelle and Lydia learned quickly and then Bret taught them to dive off the rock. Little Anne was another story. She did not like to put her face in the water and the lessons went a lot slower. Sarah confided in Bret that she seemed to have an unnatural fear of water. Sometimes Sarah had her lie down on the kitchen counter so she could wash her hair in the sink with the sprayer. It was so much easier than fighting her in the bathtub where she panicked if the water ran over her face.

"She will be okay," Bret assured his wife. "She just needs a little more time."

Bret put a tree swing with a board seat in the maple tree. It swung over the slope of the lawn. Just after it was installed, the manager's son Michael who was about twelve-years-old made a rope swing over next to the brook. It swung off a ledge high over the water, but only the older kids could use it. Anne and Lydia could not even reach the knot at the end.

The summer was filled with magic. Fireflies filled the air on warm evenings and were captured in jars to make lanterns. Thunderstorms rolled in and the family would unplug the television and turn off the lights, to stand on the large screened porch and watch the show. They all counted "one Mississippi, two Mississippi, three Mississippi,..." between the lightning and thunder to track the storm's progress and know when it was almost there, right over them, and moving away. The wide screened porch offered respite from the mosquitos and blackflies and became an important living space in the summer months.

When the seasons changed, the porch became the place to cool berry and apple pies without worrying about critters and bugs getting into them.

In the early evening, as loons called to each other across the lake, bats flew out from under the eaves at the highest peak of the house. Bret explained to the children that bats are good for keeping down mosquitos and black flies. At first there seemed to be no harm in letting them live up in the attic. But as the summer wore on, there were several incidents of bats getting into the house. The peaceful evening would erupt in running, screaming girls and Bret swinging a butterfly net through the house trying to catch the intruder. Before fall arrived, Bret went up into the attic and plugged all the holes he could find while the bats were out hunting.

Evie and Jenny discovered over the summer that Craig Pond was the hangout for kids their age. They walked the half mile up the hard packed dirt road through the woods and spent much time there meeting people they would be going to school with at Bucksport High in the fall. Isabelle started second grade at Orland Elementary. The three of them caught the early morning bus, in the dark during December and January. The hatchery kids were the first pickup for the rural route and the last drop off at the end of the day. Isabelle sometimes fell asleep on the way home.

Sarah set up an account with Wight's Dairy for fresh milk delivery each week into the box by the front door. A waxed cardboard cover sealed each glass bottle. Rinsed empty bottles left in the box were picked up at the next delivery. With so many kids in the house, Sarah stretched the budget by adding powdered milk and water to the bottles when they reached half full. The milkman was afraid of old Bow, who had never encountered such a thing. She barked at the man because of his unfathomable fear. She never in her life growled, much less bit anyone.

Evie turned seventeen that fall and found a job waiting tables at Alamoosook Lodge on the other side of the lake. She took the car to work and liked having her own money to spend. One evening the cook went out to the garbage shed and found a large raccoon in it making a mess. He came in to get a shotgun and killed the masked bandit. Just then, he spotted two sets of eyes in the woods shining red in the ray from the flashlight. The adult raccoon had been a mother with two tiny babies. They all stood around feeling bad wondering what to do. In the end, the dishwasher took one home and Evie brought the other home.

When she walked in the door, she found her parents in the living room watching *Gunsmoke*. Everyone else was in bed. She walked up to her mother and slowly lowered the zipper on her jacket to reveal the tiny masked face.

"Oh, no. What on earth," Sarah said under her breath. Bret got up from his chair and walked across the room.

"Oh...." he said, and gently took the baby animal from Evie's hands. She explained what had happened and they all started talking about how to feed it. Sarah found a bottle from when the kids were younger and put some milk on the stove to warm it. She sat with the baby in her lap and it fed voraciously from the bottle.

"What now?" Sarah asked.

Bret thought. "We cannot keep a wild animal without a permit. And shots." He paced the floor nervously smoking a cigarette.

"Well, for now, the little thing seems content and well-fed," Sarah said. It snuggled into her lap and fell sound asleep. "Go to bed," she told Evie. "We will find a bed for the baby."

Together, she and Bret found one of the smaller moving boxes in the garage, put a towel in the bottom and placed it on the floor register in their dining room. The next day, Cleo called the regional office and put Bret on the phone with a wildlife warden. It was possible to obtain a permit to keep the raccoon and raise it to adulthood, which seemed like the humanitarian thing to do. Neutering and rabies shots would be required.

When he told Sarah about his findings the next evening, she replied, "What a very Maine-like thing for us to under-take," and they both smiled at each other.

Early the next morning the kids dubbed the new addition Cooney. He went to the vet for shots and neutering. The vet said it was the highlight of his career to unexpectedly venture into wildlife care. Thus, the family grew once again.

Bret spent much effort building a zoo-worthy enclosure in the garage with a floor to ceiling wooden frame with screening over and a climbing tree inside. As it turned out, Cooney found a way to escape out the top and live in the pigeon coop above the garage. The kids adored him, but he bonded with Sarah who was his surrogate mother.

Once he could eat solid food, it was dry dog food and table scraps. He made a big mess on the kitchen floor washing every bite in the water bowl with much splashing. Sarah moved the food and water bowls to opposite corners of the room, which only resulting in him taking each bite over across the floor for washing, making an even bigger mess. Everyone was fascinated watching his hands carefully wash each item.

That winter he trailed along behind her and the kids on long walks. Sometimes, he got as worn-out as Anne did, and Sarah had to carry both of them back home. Whenever he was frightened by a loud noise or unknown dog he climbed up Sarah's legs to snuggle under her collar at the back of her neck.

A lot of snow fell that winter. Storm after storm deposited snow plowed into four-foot banks on the edge of roads. Cooney was allowed in the house to visit and once he startled the cat who ran straight up the Christmas tree. Before anyone could intervene, Cooney went up the tree as well and the whole thing crashed onto the floor. Bret wired the tree to the wall after that and for many years thereafter.

The family bought a toboggan for Christmas and they all squeezed on board for trips down the packed snow road to the lake. Cooney was right in the middle of this activity and rode inside the curl at the front. The best ride was when the toboggan successfully made the turns by everyone leaning hard the right way, and it would sail right out onto the frozen lake. Sarah made hot cocoa with marshmallows to warm them when they all came in with red noses and cold feet.

In the dead of winter, the ice was thick enough to drive on and people came to ice fish. Bret made a sleigh to haul the equipment, and sometimes Anne, out onto the lake. He made a fire on the shore for them to keep warm while he caught fresh fish for dinner.

That whole winter, Lydia and Anne were home with Sarah during the weekdays. Without any big sisters to monitor the interaction between them, Lydia got an attitude. She decided that she would like to have the undiluted attention of her mother. To bring this point home, she started being mean to Anne. One day it might be taking her cookie away from her when no one was looking. Another day it might be calling her stupid, but it became an everyday habit. Isabelle was very keen to see this and prevent it when they were all together. Somehow, Lydia made sure her mother never saw anything, making Anne seem like a crybaby. The three young girls formed a pattern between them. Isabelle was the moderator, keeping everything civil. It only took a moment for chaos to ensue when Lydia and Anne were alone.

Beyond this, Lydia was becoming difficult in other ways. One day when the three little girls sat together eating fish sticks, Lydia declared she would not eat hers and hid them in the bookcase. Another day, without warning, she dumped her glass of orange juice over Anne's head. Sarah was watching now but unsure what to do. Bret noted that among the younger girls, she was the middle child, and sometimes that alone caused behavior problems.

When spring came, the ice on the lake cracked and shifted with huge booming noises. Cooney had grown considerably. He trailed after Sarah all day and his favorite activity was hanging laundry on the line. He would jump in the basket of wet laundry, grab choice items and run up the hill into the woods with them. Sometimes he even pulled them down off the clothesline. Sarah would inevitably retrieve them and usually have to rewash them, but never without a sense of humor.

As Cooney grew, his temperament began to change. The kids would jump up on the sofa to avoid nipped toes when he ran through the living room. As it turned out the neighbors had a large Siamese cat with a remarkably bad temper. Cooney and the cat fraternized with each other, and one day Sarah saw the two of them walking off under the juniper bushes and into the woods. They were never seen again and the story held that Cooney grew up and ran away with the neighbor's cat.

Evie and Jenny babysat sometimes. Evie was kind and caring, but Jenny was deep in the throes of adolescent hormonal chaos. The younger girls learned to avoid her. And the crazy behavior of Lydia went on unabated. Isabelle kept her littlest sister close when she could to keep her safe from Lydia's abuses.

This pattern affected Anne deeply. She became more and more quiet and stopped eating. Sarah felt strongly that it was counterproductive to indulge the whims of a picky eater, but Anne was small and underweight for her age and it was starting to look like a problem. Sometimes Sarah would try to shame Anne into eating by treating her like a baby. She would put Anne in her crib and spoon-feed her, though she was much too old for that. Anne saw right through the ruse and continued to refuse all but a few bites.

There was more than just the menace of Lydia and a general feeling of foreboding. Anne thought her parents, especially her mother, was sneaking inedible things into the food. For instance, the alleged onions and mushrooms, which were bad enough, could easily be worms and slugs. Sarah found the book *Bread and Jam for Francis* at the library and read it to Anne thinking that would do the trick. It was about a little bear who would only eat bread and jam, thus missing out on all the varied cuisines of the world. But all Anne learned was that there were others who felt just like her. She felt vindicated and possibly finally understood. It was exacerbating for Sarah.

Jenny got her driver's license and she and Evie were out together a lot. The younger girls watched in fascination as they curled their hair with large rollers. Then Jenny would iron hers between sheets of waxed paper to remove its tendency to frizz. They wore mascara and short miniskirts and boyfriends would pick them up for dates. Most often, they went to visit other girls at their houses.

Evie enrolled in Physics for the fall term and was informed that this science class was not for young ladies. Enraged,

Sarah went to the principal and reminded him that Evie was a straight A student. There was no reason for denying her entry to the class. She won the argument and the principal reluctantly let her take the class, where, once again, she earned an A grade, graduating valedictorian of her class. Meanwhile, Jenny could not seem to stay out of trouble at school. She received demerits for being late to school, skipping class, smoking in the girl's room and wearing her skirts too short. She despised the administration and often came home furious and frustrated. Sarah gave Jenny support and suffered with her through her adolescent hell.

Bret worried about Jenny's attitude, but each time he tried to talk to her about it, she retreated in anger. Nonetheless, Bret loved fatherhood. He asked the manager if he could use the scrap wood from the pallets the fish food came on to make a toy box for the kids. He carefully selected boards and removed their old nails to build a large square box with a hinged lid that closed with a hasp. Best of all he went to Western Auto and bought fire engine red paint to finish the project. It was the centerpiece of the toy room. Though it could not hold all of their toys, it made a big difference in keeping things somewhat cleaned up.

That same winter, in his free time, he made bunk beds for Isabelle and Lydia. He found posts in the junk yard and used a rasp to shape them, then painted them with dark wood stain. He scavenged bedsprings at the dump and the mattresses that had moved with them sat on top. Sarah could not imagine where he found all the energy after work. Bret was so happy to be a father. He remembered how his father made him feel special and sought to do the same for his children.

When summer came around again, the yard filled with dandelions and buttercups. The younger children picked bouquet after bouquet to give to their mother until every available vessel in the house was filled with yellow tufts. Evie and Jenny needed clothes to fit in at high school, so Sarah taught them to sew. They bought patterns and fabric in the basement of Trewergy's Five and Dime Store. The sewing room became the center of activity as skirts and blouses were crafted under Sarah's guidance.

Lydia started Kindergarten in the fall, and then it was just Anne home with Sarah all day. When it was nice outside, Anne played in the back yard where Sarah could see her from the kitchen window. She was allowed to stand on a chair in the kitchen and watch what ingredients Sarah used. This went a long way in helping her eat better. She examined the ingredients closely, smelling and touching them. Some of the terrible ingredients turned out to be not so bad. When encountered in a cooked state, it helped to remember them in their raw state, much less intimidating. The best fun was when Sarah made a special treat of cookies or a cake and Anne got to lick batter and frosting from the beaters. Afternoon naps together were part of their routine.

When Sarah sat in the living room to read, Anne knew it was quiet time. She liked to wander the house and find special places to sit and listen to the stillness. One of these places was the top of the front stairs. A window high above the landing let in lots of light and the golden wood of the steps and banister were warm and inviting. Anne never felt

alone in the house. When the structure shrank and contract-
ed or warmed and expanded, it made gentle noises. Anne
decided the house was talking to her.

Sarah would quietly tiptoe through the house looking for
Anne and find her sitting perfectly still all alone on the stairs.
No toys, no words. Just sitting, listening. Sarah noted this
characteristic and wondered at its meaning. She concluded
that Anne had a lot to think about and needed space and
time to work out the mysteries of being four years old.

The next year, Sarah encouraged her older girls at sixteen
and eighteen to look for work in the summer tourist town of
Bar Harbor. They found a small affordable apartment there
for two months and the owners of Testa's Seafood Restaurant took them under their wing. They made good money
waiting tables at the wildly popular diner and acquired a
taste for fresh lobster. They saved for college and enjoyed
freedom without parental supervision. Evie would be off to
the University of Maine in the fall.

With Evie and Jenny living in Bar Harbor, it was just Sarah
and the little kids all day long. Taking Bret's cue, she told
them to go play in the woods. Together with the neighbor
boys, they climbed trees and went barefoot, coming home
with their hands and clothes black with pitch and their feet
black as tar. They gorged themselves on wild crab apples,
chokecherries, and blackberries that grew by the brook,
and chewed sweet teaberry leaves. One day they crawled
through the underbrush into the thick woods up the hill and
discovered the old apple orchard. Grown over with thick
trees, it was not possible to stand up straight, but the sunlight
filtered through to reveal golden sweet yellow apples. An-

other day they discovered grey natural clay along the bank of the creek and used it to model animals. Sarah made them scrub their hands before dinner and wash their feet in the claw foot bathtub before getting into bed.

Bret made a low bench/step stool to help the little ones reach the bathroom sink for tooth brushing. He painted colorful designs on it in red, yellow, blue and green. Sarah tucked them into bed with a kiss and wishes for sweet dreams.

One night that summer, Bret came and woke them up to put on their shoes in their nightgowns and come to the woods. There they experienced the luminescent wonder of Jack-O-Lantern Mushrooms shining orange in the dead of night. Then later that summer, a mountain lion screamed up on Great Pond Mountain late after dark. The children stood in the garage with the light on and door open looking out into the black woods. The lion seemed loud, large, close and terrifying. But Bret assured them it was a long way away and they were all safe. It burned an impression into their souls and their minds of the wonder and fierceness of the wild woods.

Less terrifying but equally fascinating were the turtles and frogs that lived in abundance around them. A box turtle came to live with them for a while, which Anne named Bocky. He ate raw vegetables scraps leftover from the meal preparation. Anne told him "good boy. Eat your vegetables." Bret enjoyed teaching his children about nature just as his father had taught him. In addition, he prepared them for school by teaching numbers and letters as soon as they could understand. He would sit in his favorite living room chair with Anne in his lap and slowly and carefully draw each letter and say words starting with it. He drew them in cursive also to show how they could be made fancy.

When fall approached, Sarah took Anne to the school to assess if she was ready to start kindergarten. She would not turn five until November, but Isabelle had started early and maybe Anne could too. Sarah and the evaluator talked together while Anne stood behind her mother's chair. When the woman asked Anne to come forward and talk to her, Anne became overwhelmed with shyness. She had very little experience with interacting beyond her immediate family and the neighbor children. This interview seemed all too solemn and important. In the end, the evaluator judged her too young and recommended another year at home.

This was disappointing for Sarah. She loved her children and would never regret her large family, but she was feeling ready for something new. She envied her oldest daughter and was thinking about perhaps going to college herself. She had not yet talked to Bret about it, but thought he would be supportive. For now it would have to wait until she got this little girl grown some more.

They settled into a routine during the school year. Sarah was up early to raise the others from their sleep. Six months out of the year, this was before daybreak. Weekdays were a sort of organized chaos. Children looking for matching socks, hair akimbo needing brushing, vying to stand over the floor grate to dress in the sole warmth in the cold house. Mostly everyone was half-asleep, grumpy and unable to even consider food. Sarah made the children drink orange juice with fluoride drops in it. Inevitably, this came after tooth brushing with Crest so the orange juice tasted terrible and left a bad taste all morning. They had to be at the hatchery office to catch the bus by 7:15 at the latest. At least they had a warm place to stand and wait, though it reeked of fish food meal, which was just more fish.

But on weekends, things were great. Everyone got to sleep as long as they wanted. And when they woke up, Sarah would be in the kitchen making something mouthwatering. Often it was French toast, pancakes, or waffles. Waffles were the best. She had two cast iron electric waffle makers, one rectangular and one round. These waffles were slathered in real sweet cream butter and genuine maple syrup, whenever possible. Despite the extra cost, supporting the local dairy and maple syrup industry was reward in itself. There were fresh berries in the summer and bananas or canned peaches or pears in the winter. Sometimes she made omelets stuffed with sautéed vegetables and cheese. Sarah stood in the kitchen and kept making them until everyone had their fill. There was also always either bacon or sausage, carefully rationed.

After these wonderful breakfast feasts on weekend morning, Sarah's efforts focused on dinners during the week. She shopped carefully trying to squeeze the very best meals out of their budget. Sarah picked up women's magazines at the grocery store and read the recipes in them, then made them better. She would rather make something rich and delicious and dole it out in smaller servings, than make large quantities of things that filled the belly but not the senses. Spices were sometimes expensive but they were the key to infusing flavor into everything she made. She found Indian spices that reminded Bret of his time there, Mexican spices, Italian herbs, and Middle Eastern flavors. Sometimes she would drive all the way to Bangor to look for herbs and spices in specialty shops. She also found some sources for mail order ingredients.

Her cooking was in sharp contrast to the subsidized hot lunch at Orland School, which cost students thirty-five cents a week. The menu was equally predictable with Bubble and Squeak, which was the term for vegetable soup with hamburger in it, nothing like British Bubble and Squeak of fried potatoes and cabbage from which the name derived.

Other predictable items were greasy skin-on baked chicken and boiled hot dogs, greasy as well. Pizza squares were cut from sheets of dough with a skiff of tomato sauce and a sprinkle of cheese. The way some of the kids devoured their own, plus whatever they could talk anyone else out of, was noteworthy. Sadly, it looked like they did not get well fed at home. This was not surprising where people living in shacks with no central heat often had the newest snowmobiles. It was a different social structure with unusual values. But never did neighbors dare judge the treatment of others' children.

Nor' Easta'

A S THE TREES TURNED brilliant red, orange, and yellow, Sarah turned her thoughts to cozy indoor activities. She invited John's wife Mary over for coffee. They did not see each other much, but today Sarah needed some company. Everyone on hatchery road shared a party line. You never answered it until you heard the ringtone for your house, a unique combination of long and short rings. Though there were eight households on the line, the four on the hatchery property had to go through a special procedure to call each other: dial the four-digit number, then hold down the receiver until it stopped ringing, signaling that the other party had picked up. Then pick the receiver back up and hope they had not given up and disconnected.

Mary came over and once they sat down at the table with hot mugs of coffee, Mary reported news that a "Nor' Easta" (Northeaster) was on its way.

"Oh, does that mean wind from the Northeast?" Sarah asked.

"It's more than that. Storms coming from that direction pick up moisture from the sea. A Nor' Easta' is always a big deal," Mary said. They paused, Sarah envisioning torrential rain and ice. "But on the other side of this storm it will be time to gather balsam for wreathes," Mary told her in her deep accent.

"You make wreaths?" Sarah asked.

"Oh yes. Been making them since I learned as a girl. I can teach you if you want to learn. Lots of us around here do it and then sell them to a man who takes them to the city," Mary told her.

"What city? Portland?"

"No, he goes all the way down to Boston where he can get top dollar," Mary said.

"Really? Hey have you ever thought about taking them to Boston yourself and keeping all that money?" Sarah was getting excited.

"No, I don't make enough wreaths on my own to be worth the trip," Mary said.

"What if you and I work together to make as many as the station wagon will hold and go to Boston ourselves to sell them? It would be extra money for Christmas," Sarah said.

"I would not enjoy a winter trip to Boston, but I suppose I could help you make as many as you like to take down there," Mary said thoughtfully. "We can't spare our truck, but you could use our trailer with your car."

"Great! I can't wait to get started," Sarah said.

They moved on to talking about sewing and Sarah gave Mary a few dress patterns to try. By the time the kids were home from school an icy wind had picked up that rattled the windows all evening and into the night. When they woke in the morning, ice covered the world outside. Tree limbs hung nearly to the ground, while others had come down and shattered in the road. It was nearly impossible to walk outside, much less drive. Sarah turned on the radio and heard that all the schools in the state closed. Then about an hour later, the electricity and phone lines went down.

Bret slipped, slid and skated over to the office and took care of essential tasks related to the care of the smaller fish. Then he made his way back shivering in the icy wind.

"Oh boy. This is bad. I need to try and get that old wood stove up here from the basement in case we are without heat for days," he told Sarah.

Though the stove was on the small side, it was nonetheless solid cast iron. He made a skid out of boards and tied tow straps around the stove. He tied the other end to the porch post out the window at the top of the stairs. As he moved it a few inches at a time up the skid, Sarah stood at the post and pulled up the slack around the post while Bret rested for a moment. At last, the stove made it up to the kitchen. Bricks from a small pile out in the back yard made a hearth to set the stove on by the kitchen chimney. Bret called the neighbors and tracked down some stovepipe that he ventured out to collect and haul home.

With the stove ready to go, he took the sled out to collect wood, starting with what had broken and fallen in the road. Between the chainsaw and ax, he had a pile of useable wood and the fire going by mid-afternoon. The house was about forty-five degrees by then, but the kitchen was soon very warm. Sarah heated water on the wood stove for coffee and hot chocolate, and made a pot of stew. After dark, Sarah lit candles and they all sat in the kitchen playing checkers and cards in the dim light.

When it was time for the kids to go to bed, they crawled between the cold sheets in their flannel nightgowns. An hour later when Sarah checked on the girls, she found Isabelle, Lydia, and Anne all cuddled together in Isabelle's bed for warmth. She felt bad she had not remembered the hot water bottles. She filled one for Jenny and one for herself and Bret to share. They all slept deeply.

Two days later, with power restored, school resumed. The woodstove would become a necessary backup for future storms from the ominous North Atlantic.

After that, the weather settled down until November 1, when the sky started dropping large fluffy snowflakes. It was beautiful. The snow just kept coming. Sarah filled the bird feeders outside the kitchen window with seeds and suet. A bird book and notepad sat on the windowsill for identifying and recording birds seen at the feeder. Winter regulars included chickadees, nuthatches, cardinals, snow buntings, and even an enormous pileated woodpecker. As the day progressed, beautiful frost patterns covered the windows, which fascinated the girls. It snowed all night and into the next day accumulating three feet.

When the sun finally came out, Mary called and said it was time to collect balsam. Sarah cleared out the sewing room to make table space for them to work. The two of them, with Anne in tow, bundled up in their warmest winter clothes and drove in Mary's truck to a place along the road to town. They trudged through the drifts into the woods to cut the fragrant boughs and filled the truck bed.

When all the greenery was unloaded into the sewing room through the mudroom entrance, Mary went back over to her house to fetch the wreath rings, wire, and ribbon she had sent for weeks before. She also brought a large basket of pinecones she had collected in the fall. They wore gloves to prevent blisters, but also to keep their hands free of sticky sap. First, she showed Sarah how to trim the branch tips to the right length, then how to wire them onto the rings, leaving a hanging loop at the top, and lastly how to make the bows and attach pinecones for decoration. They worked for two days and made three sizes. The entire house smelled heavenly.

When they were finished and all the good bough tips used, they loaded the wreathes into Sarah's station wagon. Then John helped her hitch up the trailer and they filled that as well. After dinner, Sarah cleared out the sticky sappy mess of limbs and needles tracked throughout the downstairs.

The next morning, she got the kids to the hatchery office at 7:00 to wait for the bus. She waved to Bret on her way out as he performed the daily ritual of drawing the American flag up the pole by the office, then dropped Anne off at the Grindle's house up the road to play with their children. She set off for Boston by herself under a brilliant blue sky and nearly blinding brightness as the snow reflected the sun. Joanne Grindle would bring Anne home when Bret got off work at 4:30. Sarah drove four hours and set up a sales booth at Faneuil Hall Farmers Market. She sold out of wreathes by 6:00 p.m. and made it back home by midnight. She gave Mary a generous portion of the proceeds and stashed the rest away for Christmas presents. It was a lot of work, but a satisfying accomplishment.

A week later, Bret, Sarah, the younger girls, and Bow the beagle bundled up and traipsed up the two-track road toward the mountain to find a Christmas tree. It was the weekend after Thanksgiving. Snowmobiles had made tracks to follow that helped keep them from sinking up to their waists in snow. The trees were all so perfect that they had a hard time deciding which to cut. In the end, they cut two trees, one for the playroom and one for the dining room. They dragged them home with Bow in the lead wearing Isabelle's scarf around her neck.

They waited for Bret to untangle the strings of lights, replace burned-out bulbs and arrange them on the trees before the children helped unpack the decorations. The most precious ones were Bret's grandmother Bertha's hand-made decorations she received from her family in Germany. These included a Nativity Scene carefully arranged on the dining room bureau where table linens were stored. Anne at five years old could not remember what to call the scene and retrieved an alternate name for it from words she knew. Thus, it was christened the activity shack, which stuck thereafter.

The old house was magical at Christmas time. Sarah found electric candles on one of her foraging trips to Bangor and they adorned the front windows of the house. Approaching in the evening, the house looked like a scene from a Christmas card. Since the main living area was toward the back of the house, the front windows displayed the candle light without the distraction of electric lights. Evergreen garlands were wound around the stairway banister in the front hall.

On Christmas Eve, Bret opened the living room fireplace and lit the fire beneath their hanging stockings. The little girls had been practicing Christmas carols for weeks at Bret's encouragement. Evie was home from school and she and Jenny laughed hysterically as the kids mixed up the lyrics of the old traditional songs.

"What the heck is a Herald Angel?' Lydia asked.

"Yeh, it makes me think of Harold who works at the filling station," Isabelle mused. Harold was big and round, smelled like gasoline, and always had a huge cigar butt between his teeth. "Is he an angel? Do all angels look like that?" she speculated.

"Then there's the one about the 'round young virgin.' I guess she was a little chunky," Anne said.

On Christmas Eve, Grandma Elsie and Grandpa Eddie called from Oklahoma. The three little girls stood around the handset and sung a verse of Silent Night to them, extra loud to carry over the great distance. Dinner was clam chowder, then mounds of buttered popcorn. When the little ones were all in bed, they lay awake for hours listening to the laughter and hilarity shared by the older girls and their parents.

With the help of Sarah's wreath money, it was a huge Christmas for them all, with presents overflowing from under the tree on Christmas morning. Evie and Jenny helped Sarah prepare a dinner of beef rib roast, mashed potatoes and gravy, candied carrots, home-baked sage yeast bread, and minced meat pie. It was a lovely candlelit late afternoon meal. Ice water was made special with the good stemware and the cloth napkins were carefully arranged at each place setting. It was the last holiday meal they would all share for many years.

Picking Apples

1890: GENEVA TOLD NELL that the apples should be ripe in the meadows east of town and asked her to go pick some. As usual, she stopped at the tavern to see if Emily would join her. They walked fast enjoying the fresh air and each other's company. When they passed the graveyard, they both averted their eyes to avoid looking at the foot image on the headstone of Colonel Jonathan Buck. It was a dark curiosity that added an unwanted notoriety to their town. No one knew the true story, but there were rumors about a curse placed on the colonel by a woman. Some said they had been lovers, some said she was a witch that he killed. No one knew for sure. Hannah was a distant relative to the Buck family and had told the girls that there was definitely a woman that Colonel Buck had burned.

"So she must have been a witch, right? They used to burn witches at the stake," Emily reasoned.

"Well, you would think so, but there is no record of such a proceeding, which the Colonel would have recorded. It would have been a legal proceeding," Hannah said.

"Then what happened? Did he do it illegally?" Nell asked.

"From everything I have read and from the lore passed down through the family, the Colonel would no sooner break the law than slit his own throat," Hannah told them. "He was of the highest moral character, which is why he was given the commission to settle this place."

It was a mystery. All that they did know is that the image of the foot and lower leg appeared on the headstone shortly after it was erected and that no efforts to remove it were successful. The girls, as well as many people in town, tried to ignore it lest the curse rub off on them.

The girls found the trees heavy with apples and filled their large baskets to the top. As they picked, they chattered away to each other about nothing and everything, i.e. the thoughts of fifteen-year-old girls.

"Nell, how many children do you hope to have when you marry," Emily asked.

"Oh, I don't know. When I think of how many women die giving birth, sometimes I think it would be lucky to have none," Nell replied.

"Don't be silly. If you are married, your husband will expect you have his children," Emily said. "And mother says you have to do your duty in making your body available for your husband whenever he wants it. You can't very well choose not to."

They thought about this for a few minutes. "I can barely imagine taking off all my clothes and getting into bed with a naked man," Nell said.

"I can. In fact, I can't wait," Emily said wistfully. "Mother says it's rather fun once you get the hang of it."

"I have heard that, too. I suppose you get used to seeing each other naked," Nell said.

"I want a big family. Lots of little children to love and spoil. It sounds delightful," Emily said.

"You aren't afraid to pass a baby out from between your legs? I have heard the screaming when the midwife comes to town to attend a birth. The whole town can hear it even from the most proper women," Nell said.

"Yes, I know. But mother says it's worth it once you have a little bundle in your arms," Emily said.

"Our kids will be best friends, Emily. We will raise them together and tell them they are cousins. We just have to get our husbands to agree to live near each other," Nell said warmly.

"Agreed. We will always be best friends," Emily said.

Nell, distracted by the beautiful day and the company of her dear friend, had quite forgotten about her plans to cause mischief concerning Mr. Atkins.

I T WAS A MONTH later before Nell saw Charles again. She was on her way to buy butter from the dairy wagon that came to town every day. As she passed the livery stable, Mr. Atkins stepped out and greeted her warmly by name.

"May I walk with you?" he asked.

"Yes, of course," she smiled at him.

"How are you and your parents getting on?" he asked.

"Just fine. My mother is making a pie today and needs more butter for the crust so I am going to the dairy wagon," she said.

"Oh, pie! I love pie. What kind is she making?" he asked.

"Peach pie with vanilla ice cream," she replied.

"She must be a good cook," Charles said.

"Oh, yes. She works hard at it. And you can see that my father is well fed," she joked.

"That is true. He looks to be well cared for," he said.

They made idle banter back and forth until she arrived at the dairy wagon. After she made her purchase, he asked if he could escort her home. He became quite animated telling her about his hatchery project. She could feel his passion for what he was doing and became mesmerized by his excitement.

When they arrived at the house, Geneva saw them approaching from the kitchen window and opened the door as they approached.

"Hello, Mum. This is Mr. Atkins who offered to walk me home," Nell said.

He tipped his hat, smiled, and said, "Good day, Mrs. Chandler."

"Very pleased to meet you," Geneva said. "Welcome to our town."

"Thank you so much. With your permission, ma'am, I would like to extend an invitation to your daughter to come out to the lake with me this weekend to see the project I am building. I can bring around a buggy to pick her up," he said, and then turned to Nell and said, "That is if she is interested."

"Yes, that would be lovely," she said.

Geneva smiled warmly and said, "I can send you off with a picnic if you like."

"Splendid! I will come by at 10:00 on Saturday morning," he said as he tipped his hat and turned to walk back down the hill.

Once Nell was inside and the door was closed, Geneva grabbed her hands and said, "Oh my! He is so handsome and such a gentleman. However did this come about?"

"Emily and I ran into him about a month ago and he introduced himself. Today he joined me when I passed by the livery stable," she said with a big smile.

"I am so pleased for you, dear," her mother said.

That evening at dinner, Maynard said, "I found out whose funeral you passed by on your way to Bangor. It was young Paul Ingram. He was out cutting wood with his father and the tree fell the wrong way and crushed him. He was only seventeen years old."

"How terribly sad," Geneva said. "Just goes to show you can't take life for granted. It could end anytime for any of us."

"I agree. We must always count our blessings and be grateful for the time we have here," Maynard said solemnly.

"Well, on a happier note, Nell has been asked on an outing by Mr. Atkins," Geneva told her husband with a big smile.

"Is that right?" he said turning to Nell. "How nice of him."

"He walked her home earlier today and I met him. He is quite dashing," Geneva added.

Nell blushed, but could not contain a smile. She was, in fact, floating on air at the thought of Saturday.

When the time finally came around, Nell wore her new green and grey dress. Geneva packed them a picnic of chicken sandwiches, blueberry tarts, and a jug of fresh lemonade. It was a beautiful day without a cloud in the sky. The ride was a little over an hour and then they spent several hours hiking around as he pointed out where he wanted to build fish troughs and where might be a good place for a house and orchard someday. They sat on a blanket and had a long leisurely picnic, then talked for another hour before heading home.

Nell was utterly enchanted with Charles. When he dropped her off at her house, he walked her to the door carrying the picnic basket and kissed the back of her hand. He said he would very much like to see her again and she agreed that he could call on her.

She fell in bed that night absolutely intoxicated with the thought of him. Her parents talked in low voices in the living room.

"How very interesting that he is talking about building a house. He seems to have plans to stay here," Maynard said after hearing Geneva's report that she had pried out of Nell.

"Yes, imagine if Nell could live out there by the lake. What a fine life," Geneva said.

"Don't get ahead of yourself. He is a young man and they have only been out once. Give them time," he said.

"Oh, like you gave me time? You practically asked me to marry you the day we met," she teased.

"Well now, that was different," he said, winking at her.

"Of course. Good night you old romantic," she said as she headed up the stairs to their bed.

Charles and Nell began to see each other regularly after that. Each time he dropped her back home, he would ask about a future date to get together again. After three times, it felt most certain that they were courting. Emily would question Nell endlessly for every detail of their outings. Living vicariously through her friend was keeping Emily from feeling completely left out. Charles was the best thing to happen, even if it was not happening to her.

Nell had quite literally become a new person under the gaze of Charles. He made her feel as though she were the most beautiful, important person alive. She took more care to wash and fix her hair and put oils on her face at night to keep her skin vibrant. Love is never so strong as in the heart of a girl just turning sixteen years old.

Nell was an open book, recounting nearly every detail she could recall while gazing off into space reliving it all again. Emily asked so many questions that in the end she might just as well have been with them the entire time. Nell did not mind. She and Emily had been thick as thieves for almost their entire lives, and they intended to remain so far into the future.

The following week, the girls sat together at the kitchen table with Geneva thinking up special fare for the holidays ahead. She wanted to engage the girls in an interest in cooking, since she knew Hannah would never teach Emily anything of the sort.

"Let's come up with some special desserts we can try together. Emily, do you know of any that sound good?" Geneva asked.

"Well, once when I was in Bangor with my parents, we had supper at a nice restaurant on the waterfront. Their menu included several dessert. And though we did not order any, the descriptions made my mouth water," Emily said.

"Like what? Do you remember?" Geneva asked.

"I remember words like chocolate, brandy, orange liquor, strawberries."

"That sounds heavenly. Maybe we can buy just a small amount of liquor from the Inn and see what fruit is available. This will be fun! Maybe Charles can be lured in for taste testing." Geneva said with an inquiring look at Nell.

Emily shifted in her seat, hesitated, then suggested they try selling some desserts at the tavern to raise Christmas money.

"Yes, wouldn't that be splendid. Ask your parents if it is alright though," Geneva added.

"Of course. But I know they will be pleased," Emily said.

Hidden Treasures

A T LAST, ANNE STARTED kindergarten in 1966. Two weeks before school, Sarah and Jenny gave the kids matching pixie haircuts, short up over the ears with bangs. They went through the girls' closets and Sarah assessed where they were lacking. She went to Bangor one evening and came back with a few new things for each of them, including a soft V-neck sweater for Jenny.

Just before school started, they went to the Blue Hill Fair. Jenny declined the invitation, which was now the pattern. She wanted to be with her friends and viewed invitations to this sort of outing as a plea for additional supervision of the little girls. It was the first time the girls had experienced such a thing and Bret and Sarah wanted them to understand the significance of country fairs. They talked on the way about the long history of fairs and their purpose of celebrating the harvest, competing for honors with livestock and produce, and a festive community gathering before winter set in. As usual, there was not extra cash, so they told them in the car before they even arrived, "We have to pay for admission, but don't ask for balloons and cotton candy. All the vendors want to sell overpriced things that we cannot afford. Don't even ask."

The day was devoted to the heart of the fair. They toured livestock barns, watched oxen pulling competitions, and looked at all the sights. The girls did not ask to buy anything, but Sarah was miffed to find they had to purchase toilet paper at the restroom. A grossly overweight homely woman sat in a chair by the entrance door with a sign that read "Toilet Paper Ten Cents." Sarah resentfully paid the outrageous price for four small pieces of toilet paper for her and the girls. She vowed to start carrying toilet paper in her purse thereafter. Luckily, there was still enough money left to give the girls a surprise ride on the carousel and then a ride on the Ferris wheel. They stayed for the fireworks and went home feeling filled with the wholesome sights and sounds of the fair.

Anne could not sleep the night before school started. It was simply too exciting. When she finally slept for a few hours, it was already time to get up. She woke up feeling horrible with a headache and stiff neck. Sarah got the thermometer and found she had a low-grade fever. She missed the first day.

"Just nerves I bet," she told Bret.

Lydia had done so much to destroy Anne's self-confidence that she did not have resilience. Even when playing with the Grindle children, when she mentioned going out to their tree house, she was immediately admonished. "It's a tree *fort*, not a tree *house*! We are not playing house with you." She felt her face grow red and held back tears. No resilience.

That evening when the children were all in bed, Sarah said, "It is so interesting to me how very different all the children are. They don't look alike and they all have very different personalities. Jenny and Lydia especially stand out as fierce survivors. Where did they get that?"

Bret reasoned it out for her. "If you look back at our ancestry, including Sam's, we are all from German or Welsh stock. Vikings from the north populated those places. So, I think we are raising Vikings."

They were silent for a moment, then Sarah said, "I can see it now. The girls coming in from playing in the woods carrying spears and wearing fur clothing and helmets with horns." They both laughed.

"But what of little Anne?" Sarah asked him. "I have spent so much time worrying about her tiny size and lack of appetite. In an earlier time, I wonder if she would have survived. Now she is too neurotic to start school?"

Bret puffed on his pipe. He had switched from cigarettes to save money. After a moment of thought, he said, "Wait and see. I bet that one will surprise you."

The next morning Anne got dressed in a red hand-me-down dress, but didn't realize until she was on the bus that she still had her short pajama bottoms on underneath. The elastic around the bottom made the sides puff out under her dress. She felt ridiculous. Isabelle walked her to her classroom and introduced her to the teacher. Anne had never seen little desks just her size and felt a sense of immediate understanding as she slid into a seat.

On that second day of school they each were called up to the teacher's desk and asked to count as high as they could and say the alphabet if they knew it. Most of the other children could do neither, no matter how much prompting.

When it was Anne's turn, she said the entire alphabet and then counted to 37 before the teacher stopped her and told her she could sit back down. Much of the year was just going over the things she already knew, so her focus was on making friends. Orland Consolidated School went from kindergarten through eighth grade. Anne's class was the biggest in the whole school with thirty-two students.

There was a lot of playtime at school. Recess outside included a large space at the back of the building with eight swings that went high, a merry-go-round that you pushed, and teeter-totters. In the classroom there was singing, dancing, drawing, coloring, learning how to be still and line up, but mostly there was playing. She was not shy for long as all the kids jumped into games of make-believe. School was an awakening.

～ஒஂ

J ENNY GRADUATED FROM HIGH School that spring and was the salutatorian for her class. She was a nervous wreck about giving her speech, but managed to calm her nerves and deliver it without incident. It was a bitter struggle to accept an honor from the people she disliked so much. But now, she was done with them and done with that place.

Evie and Jenny were naturally closer to each other than to the younger girls. They had grown up together and were well aware that they had a different father, though the younger children were clueless. Jenny especially felt that she was being squeezed out that final year of high school.

"I bet everyone will be happy when they get me out of the house," she complained to Evie.

"No, don't say that," Evie told her. "It is just our time to begin our adult lives. Of course it will probably be some relief to have fewer people to feed, but it's not meant in a mean way."

"You think so? Well it will be interesting to see how things change. I bet they will help pay for college for the others even though they could not afford one cent to help us," Jenny spat.

"I don't think so. But we will see. No value in dwelling on it. Time to get on with life, right?" Evie said. "Besides, sometimes this house creeps me out. I feel like there are devils in the walls."

"I know," Jenny said. "One night I woke up and looked out the window onto the balcony and there was a huge owl sitting on the banister staring at me. Not staring out looking for something to hunt, but looking straight at me. I read somewhere owls are inhabited by the spirits of the deceased."

"See? Good time to move out," Evie replied.

Jenny laid her blue jeans out on the roof, next to the balcony to weather in the rain, wind and sun. She wore her hair loose and stopped curling and ironing it, letting it frizz out around her face in wild abandon. She left in July on a bus for Boston to attend art school. She wrote to Sarah that she found a job as a chambermaid and rented an apartment with other girls her age she found through a newspaper classified ad.

Evie continued at UMO, but did not come home for the summer. She found a job in Bangor and rented an apartment there, from which she would commute to Orono when the fall term resumed classes.

Despite Sarah's continued challenges at home, she worked to stay in touch with her older children. Jenny was usually hard to reach. She stayed in touch with Evie better than with her mother, which pained Sarah. She wanted all of her children to be happy, whatever that meant and wherever life led them.

With the older girl's rooms vacated, Isabelle moved into Evie's yellow room. But before long, she opted for Jenny's grey room with a view of the lake out over the balcony. It was expected that Lydia would want Evie's room, which was bigger than the blue nursery room. She declined. So Anne moved across the hall where her room adjoined Isabelle's.

Bret and Sarah moved the extra beds to the playroom, which would serve as a spare room for when the older girls visited, or anyone else came to stay over. Toys that were still loved went upstairs to the girls' rooms, which now had space. Sarah took the rest to the church bazaar.

The east facing windows of Isabelle and Anne's rooms showered them in early morning light. Anne lay in her bed and watched the sky lighten and the poplar tree leaves flash green and silver in the breeze. Isabelle and Anne usually left the door adjoining their rooms open. It was almost like still sharing a room.

There was a restaurant across the river from Bucksport in Prospect that John and Mary recommended to Bret. A large five-dollar bucket of steamed clams would feed the whole family.

Bret took the girls there as one of their first restaurant experiences. After going a few times, Bret and Sarah decided they should try their hand at digging their own clams. They watched the tide tables and planned for a low tide adventure along the river. They had to invest in knee-high rubber boots from Rosen's Department Store. They borrowed clam rakes from John and Mary. Rising bubbles on the gelatinous surface of the mud revealed the clam's location below. Anne was seriously worried the mud would suck her under and stayed very close to Sarah in case she needed rescuing. The washed and steamed clams provided a free dinner. Getting out the sand was the trick, and they consumed many gritty clams. Anne picked at hers and ate several pieces of bread with butter.

Bret's obsession of the season was gardening. He hand dug a large garden plot in the back yard and rented a rototiller to finish the job. He carefully laid out straight string lines according to a planting diagram penciled carefully over several evenings. All the produce was started from seeds planted by the family under close supervision by Bret. Each evening, he went to the garden to inspect, water, and pull weeds.

Later that summer they embarked on a blueberry picking adventure. Early in the morning, they set off up the mountain with a small propane camp stove, bacon and eggs, canteens of water, and picking pails that nested together by size. It was windy and cool at the top and the hot bacon and egg breakfast warmed them. They picked all morning. By the time they were ready to head down hill, the day was gloriously warm and bright under a blue sky filled with white fluffy clouds reflected in the lake below. In addition to stuffing themselves with ripe blueberries, they brought home enough for a pie, blueberry pancakes the next day, plus enough for the freezer for another pie at Thanksgiving.

Peaches were on sale at a roadside stand and Sarah bought enough for another pie. She sat in the sun outside the garage peeling them into a bowl. Bees came to lick the sweet juice from her fingers, and she worked on, undeterred. The girls sat and watched, and kept asking if she was scared.

"No. They don't want to sting me. They just want the juice," she answered.

"What does it feel like to have them walking on your hands," Isabelle asked.

"It tickles a little. But mostly I don't feel them. They weigh nothing," she answered. When she was finished and ready to enter the house, she gently brushed them off her hands, and they flew off as if there was nothing left to say. Sarah carefully made a latticed top pie, sprinkled with sugar and served with vanilla ice cream.

Over dessert, the girls told Bret about the bees. Seeing a teachable moment, he told them all about bees and their environmental importance for pollination.

"But they sting you," Anne told him.

"I know, but they only do it to protect the hive or when there is danger to themselves or other bees," he explained.

"In fact, when they sting, they give up their life. They die afterwards."

They all ate in silence for a few minutes. Then they all declared that they liked bees. Sarah and Bret smiled at each other.

The garden yielded so much produce; fresh salads were served every evening. Lettuce, spinach, cucumbers, and tomatoes were eaten daily. Shucked peas only lasted for a few meals. Squash, potatoes, and onions were stored in the pantry. The freezer was packed solid with the final harvest.

Corn was the last thing to ripen in the short Maine summer and just when it was ready raccoons raided and stole all of the ears. Bret was not upset, but rather delighted that the raccoons got the corn.

As the holidays rolled around it was strange not having Evie and Jenny there. They both sent letters saying they had other plans and hoped everyone had a nice holiday. To flesh out the party, Sarah invited the manager's family to come for Thanksgiving dinner. It was an olive branch toward Bret's sometimes-strained relationship with his boss, but for Sarah it just made it seem more festive. She made a tall centerpiece of bare branches with rose hips and cattails. The traditional turkey dinner with all the trimmings was timed around the Dallas Cowboys football game, which was a non-negotiable necessity. Aluminum foil flags draped the rabbit ear antenna, and the full blast volume explained what was undiscernible from the fuzzy picture. Just before dinner, Sarah turned on the mixer to mash the potatoes which obliterated the TV picture altogether during the final play. But the Cowboys won anyway, much to Bret's delight. He knew his father would be watching.

During Christmas break, a big snowstorm brought several feet of clean white snow and once the sun came out it turned into perfect packing snow. Snowball fights ensued with the neighbor kids and giant drifts left by the snowplow became snow forts. Isabelle had the brilliant idea to build snow horses instead of snowmen. They had a groove to use as a stirrup and were ridden for several days before deteriorating into slush.

That winter the hatchery had been having trouble with thieves stealing the large adult salmon, because they were delicious to eat. Chain link fences and motion-activated alarms were not working. Every breeze set the alarms off so they were useless. The manager decided they would rotate to do patrols through the night. This happened in the bitter cold of winter and Bret was not pleased to take his night on the hourly patrols. To keep him awake for these night duties, he took up painting. Oil paints and small canvases sat beside his living room chair next to a cup filled with various size brushes. His paintings were of colorful rainbow trout, vases catching the light, and scenes from his imagination.

One night during this bitter cold winter, Bret came upstairs, gently woke Sarah and the girls, and told them to put something on their feet and wrap up in their blankets. Then he took them all out on the balcony. There in the sky were wave after wave of green, blue, and gold northern lights. None of them had ever seen such a thing. They watched for about twenty minutes until they were all shivering. It was something they would never forget. Something beyond description. The next day when they were fully awake Bret tried to explain the phenomenon, but it made little sense to any of them. It was simply wondrous.

✦

If Wishes Were
Horses

1891: CHARLES' ATTENTIVENESS TO Nell was a balm for her soul. She was in heaven. She felt so alive and beautiful in his presence. The way he looked at her made her feel perfect in her own skin. Any doubts she ever had about her looks or character or prospects for the future disappeared under the gaze of this lovely man.

Her parents saw the difference immediately. Geneva was especially excited for her daughter and looked upon her with new eyes. Nell was becoming a woman and would soon have a home and children of her own. And what an honor it was to have a handsome, college educated man courting her daughter. She took special care to make sure Nell's dresses were laundered, pressed, and mended for her outings with Charles. She baked special treats to pack in their picnics, and encouraged Nell to get busy on her trousseau.

With Nell's newly found will and energy, the sewing circle was no longer a chore. She sat and answered questions from the other girls about Charles and about her hopes and feelings, all the while unable to hide her smile. The other girls were clearly envious. Besides Emily, there were four other girls in the circle.

Cara was sixteen and promised to the cobbler's son, Tom, who would one day take over the family business. Tom was kind and considerate, and cute in a boyish sort of way, but not very smart. At least not as smart as Cara. Laurel was a large round girl, also sixteen, but without a suitor. Mabel and Harriet were both fifteen and eyeing the local boys with an interest that Emily and Nell could never muster.

Nell began a quilt of her own using dark blues and white in a star pattern. She stayed up late into the night working on it and dreaming of her future life with Charles. Her mother insisted she pay more attention in the kitchen and learn to cook, a necessary skill for a wife.

Emily and Nell worked side by side with Geneva to create mouthwatering confections and pastries to sell at the tavern. They let everyone know just before Thanksgiving that they would have a large selection ready for sale. The evening of the sale, the tavern was full as the town turned out to support the effort. It was on this occasion that Emily gathered her nerve to expose the townspeople of her lovely singing voice. She stood on an upturned beer barrel so everyone could see her and so her voice would carry to all the corners of the room. She sang Amazing Grace, The Yellow Rose of Texas, and Onward Christian Soldiers.

Nell was listening with pride for her new friend, when she noticed the look on Charles face. He seemed utterly enthralled with Emily's enchanting voice. Nell tried singing with Emily a few times when they were younger and they found she had a hard time controlling her pitch. After some embarrassment and laughter, they both agreed then that Nell was not much of a singer. At this moment her affection for her friend drifted away, replaced with envious jealousy. She tried to refocus. After all, she had the most charming eligible bachelor as her escort that night and he had complemented her elaborately on the pastries he had tried.

The next week, Nell and Charles were walking arm in arm through town and Charles asked, "Nell, darling, do you like to dance."

"I have only been to one dance and that was just before graduation. It was fun, but I hardly knew what to do. Neither did the boys though, so we all laughed and fumbled through it," Nell said.

"Was it a contra dance?" he asked.

"Yes, I believe that is what they call it. Two lines and everyone does the same steps in time."

"It just takes practice. We had them regularly at my college. There is one planned next weekend at the East Orland grange hall. Shall we attend?" he asked.

"Yes, I will give it another try," and she smiled at the thought of an evening out.

"Do you want to ask your friend Emily to join us? Perhaps I can find a partner for her," he said.

"You are so thoughtful. I am sure she will want to come, if someone has not asked her already. I will see her tomorrow at our sewing circle and ask her. Thank you. You are always so kind," she said. She smiled up into his eyes and he returned the expression of complete happiness.

When Nell told her mother, Geneva immediately started pulling Nell's dresses out to see which one she should wear and if it needed laundering or mending. Her excitement for Nell was palpable.

"I remember going to a dance with your father when we were first courting," Geneva reminisced. "We had so much fun and that was the night I knew for sure that he was the one. There is something about the music, dancing, dark of evening, and the stars in the sky that bring out the romantic in everyone."

She looked over at Nell who was brushing her long hair in the mirror. "Perhaps he will ask for your hand that night. You must be ready. Do not hesitate, but also do not act surprised. He has already set the stage by seeing you continuously for almost six months."

Nell smiled at her mother in the mirror and then blushed deeply.

"Don't worry, dear. I will tell you everything you need to know about being married. Before you know what has happened, it will all be second nature," Geneva reassured her.

Together they chose a pale blue dress with three-quarter sleeves, and a skirt overlay that opened in the front in light blue and dark blue stripes.

"Even though this is a country dance, I am going to lower the neckline on this to look more like a ball gown. You have a lovely neck that should not be hidden all the time," Geneva said.

Her hair would be set in ringlet curls around her face and tied up in the back with a large dark blue ribbon bow. She would wear her black boots, but Geneva would sew blue ribbons around the top of the boot ankle to tie in front, also in a bow. She would wear Geneva's pearl necklace that had been her grandmother's, and small pearl drop earrings.

The next day, she met Emily at the sewing circle. It was always at Laurel's house because her mother was the town's best seamstress and coached them when they were stuck on their projects. She also had a large drawing room that could accommodate all the girls. Emily had finished her quilt and they were now working on embroidering flowers and birds on linen pillowcases. The many colors of embroidery floss lay between them on a small table. They both sat in rocking chairs holding their embroidery hoops.

"I want to add some bees around my flowers," Nell said.

"Bees? Really? Whatever for? They will make you have dreams of being chased and stung," Emily said.

"No, they won't. I like bees," Nell said. "They drone around minding their own business and pollinating the flowers. I think they are sweet. Besides, my design needs some yellow."

They worked in silence for a while listening to the idle chatter of the other girls. Then one of the girls mentioned the contra dance.

"Oh, gosh I almost forgot! Charles asked if you would like to accompany us on Saturday night. The dance is out in East Orland. He said he could find you a partner, unless you already have one in mind," Nell said.

"How sweet of him," Emily said with a smile. "I would love to come along. And, no, I do not have anyone in this town that interests me in the least."

"But you have to have a partner to dance. An odd number will not do. I will ask Charles if he knows anyone," Nell said.

The other girls were also hoping to go to the dance. Cara would be there with Tom, but the others did not have dates.

Mabel sighed deeply and quoted a nursery rhyme, "If wishes were horses, beggars would ride."

After a moment, Emily said, "Hey! I have an idea. How about I bring Laurel as my date, and Mabel and Harriet can go together? Why not? No one will care. That way we don't have to worry about awkward rides home with boys we don't ever want to see again. Why get their hopes up?"

They all started talking at once and thought it was a great idea. Harriet would ask her father to drive her and Mabel out in their buggy, since Charles' buggy would only accommodate four. Nell saw Charles on Friday and told him the plan. He laughed and said it sounded like great fun, and so it was settled. When Nell told her mother that they were all going, Geneva rolled her eyes to the heavens and said, "You foolish girl. How on earth can Charles propose marriage to you if you aren't alone with him?"

"Oh, mother. It probably wouldn't have happened anyway." Nell said dismissively. "Don't worry. Time will take care of itself," and she leaned over and kissed her mother's cheek.

❧

O N Saturday evening at 6:00, Charles came by to pick up Nell who sat beside him in the front seat. They then went to Laurel's house where Laurel's mother was helping both Laurel and Emily get ready. They wore their finest gowns, Laurel in burgundy and Emily in deep emerald green. They chatted excitedly all the way there and followed other wagons going to the dance. As they approached, they heard the fiddlers practicing and saw a woman carrying a large tray of cakes and cookies for the refreshment table.

Charles helped Nell down and then assisted Laurel and Emily. As he went to park the wagon and tie the horses, the girls stood and watched the other couples arriving. It was splendid to see everyone wearing their best clothing for the event.

Nearly every single person joined the first dance. Charles and Nell stood opposite each other, with Laurel and Emily making up their four-square. A caller went over the steps quickly with everyone before the dance began. There were missteps, apologies and laughter, but soon everyone was moving together in time to the music and the calls.

After two dances both Nell and Laurel sat in chairs along the wall to rest and catch their breath, while Charles and Emily continued dancing.

"Charles is a good dancer," Laurel said.

"Yes, he knows the dances a lot better than we do," and they both laughed at themselves.

As they sat and talked, Nell watched Charles and Emily. The next dance was a waltz and they spun around the floor elegantly. Charles was completely engrossed in the dancing and gazed into Emily's eyes looking content. When they spun past and Nell saw the look on Emily's face of utter rapture, she started to feel uneasy. When the music stopped, Charles bowed low to Emily and kissed the back of her

hand. Nell scowled despite herself. She feigned content-
ment throughout the rest of the evening, as Charles danced
with her, Emily, and Laurel in turn. It was not what she
had envisioned. And definitely not what her mother had
envisioned.

The ride home was a bit somber, everyone lost in their
own thoughts. They dropped Laurel off, then Emily. Charles
helped each down from the carriage. She noticed he took
Laurel's hands, but put his hands on Emily's waist to lift her
down. When he dropped Nell off, he reached for her hands.
She hesitated, looked hard at him, then took his hands. She
slept restlessly that night feeling the ground beneath her had
shifted.

The next day, Emily was all smiles and joking with her
parents.

"Someone had a good time last night," Hannah teased.
"Tell us all about it."

"It was lovely. I wish I could do it all over again," Emily said
wistfully.

"Did you meet any interesting young men?" Hannah asked.

"No, we all just danced with Charles."

"Ah, well, that in itself would make for a fine evening,"
Hannah said and winked at Emily.

⁂

Out in the World

1966: THE COST OF heating fuel was high, but when paired with a house built in 1897 with no insulation, it was almost impossible to keep warm at any cost. The wood stove kept the kitchen warm but did not radiate beyond its doorways. Rather than incur an unpayable debt, they set the thermostat low and everyone learned to wear thick socks and sweaters. Afghans draped the living room furniture for covering shoulders and knees. The worst part was getting up in the morning. The girls took turns standing over the floor vent in the dining room to get out of their flannel nightgowns and into school clothes. Once on the school bus, the relative warmth made them sleepy, but the classroom was worse. The building was overheated and to keep students awake, the windows were opened to let in fresh air.

When the girls were younger, they generally stayed home on Saturdays while Sarah did the weekly shopping. No matter what project Bret was working on, he stayed within earshot of the kids. Sarah did not need or want the distraction of children while she shopped. She actually enjoyed a reprieve each week. Now that the kids were all in school and being properly socialized in public, she decided they could come with her if they wanted to, which they always did.

The grocery store was directly across the street from the infamous headstone of Colonel Jonathan Buck, founder of Bucksport. His grandchildren erected the headstone in the 1850s to honor him, and shortly thereafter, a distinct lower leg and foot outline appeared on the stone. Though reputable stonemasons asserted it was a natural vein of iron causing the outline, intriguing legends suited the historic town, long inhabited by descendants of the original settlers. It brought tourists and piqued children's imaginations.

It was interesting for the kids to see all the things that were available at the Shop N' Save. There were vegetables they had never seen and packages of food that never appeared in their home. The shopping choices were Sarah's alone which fell in the middle between budget constraints and her creative ideas. If the girls were good and stayed out of Sarah's way while she shopped, they were able to choose a candy bar, a decadent pleasure.

Every so often, there might be an additional stop in town at the five and dime store, or the hardware store. But in summer, the ice cream booth was open. It served soft serve vanilla or chocolate ice cream in three sizes, five cents, ten cents, or fifteen cents. The girls got ten cent cones, being not the smallest, but also not outrageous. Modest cones. Before long through rumors at school, they discovered Crosby's, which was a drive in with both soft serve and hard scoop ice cream, elevating the experience to a new level. Isabelle in her maturity of fifth grade ordered hard scoop pistachio, exotic in its green color. Lydia stuck with chocolate soft serve, and Anne graduated to vanilla chocolate twist.

This was a delightful treat but also created a desire for other things from town. One of these was Italian sandwiches, premade and wrapped in plastic wrap, sitting right by the register in Tozier's Market at one end of town and Snowman's at the other end. These small stores were open late into the night and early in the morning to serve the mill shift changes. This was the period where small mom-and-pop grocers were struggling to survive against the big chain stores, and served the need later to be filled by convenience stores. They sold some grocery essentials, beer, candy, and Italians. It was common to see millworkers just getting off the night shift buying beer at 7:30 a.m. Sarah would not buy her kids Italian sandwiches, citing unsanitary preparation areas and better food at home.

The weekend party crowd, as well as the town drunks, had two places to go. The first was the historic Jed Prouty Hotel, which included a restaurant and lounge. The other option was the Crow's Nest. They served pizza, beer nuts, hard alcohol and an occasional bar fight. Sarah and Bret were homebodies. They liked to have a few in the evening, but always in their own home.

It may have been sheer imagination fed by tales heard at school, but Lydia had a profound experience one night. In the middle of the night, the house dark except for the slight illumination from the night light in the hall to the bathroom, Lydia saw something. In the morning, while getting her shoes on for school she appeared deep in thought.

"Mum," Lydia said, then nothing followed. Sarah was doing several things at once to get them out the door on time, but did notice the long pause.

"What is it, Lydia?" she asked.

Another long pause.

"Did you come in by my bed last night?"

"Yes, when I said goodnight, remember?"

"No. Not then, but later. Late last night," Lydia said it quietly out of earshot of the others.

Sarah stopped and looked at Lydia. "No, honey. Why?"

"Nothing. I need lunch money," Lydia said, clearly changing the subject.

"Yes, okay. I will get it." Sarah said and went to her purse.

That evening, she went up to Lydia's room when it was almost time for lights out. "Do you want to tell me what happened that you asked if I came in your room last night?"

Lydia stopped looking in her drawer for warm socks to wear to bed and stared at her mother.

"What? Tell me," Sarah asked.

"Well, I just woke up and there was a woman standing by my bed dressed all in black." She glanced at her mother to see how this was being received. Sarah looked on with steady reserve. "At first I was scared, but then I relaxed and felt like it was okay. She must be a ghost, right?"

Sarah chose her words carefully. "I have never seen a ghost, but I have always felt that we are not alone here in this house." After a moment she said, "You do not have to be afraid. Let's plan to look into it this weekend, okay?"

"Okay," Lydia said.

Just to make sure, Sarah added as she turned off the light, "If you are ever afraid call me and I will be here in an instant."

"I know, Mum. Goodnight"

"Goodnight, angel."

That Saturday, Sarah took the girls to the hatchery office where they had arranged to look through the file cabinets of old photographs of the property. Because it was the weekend, there was only one person on duty, and they were working outside. They had the place to themselves and took stacks of files into the conference room. Most of what they found were old documents of little interest to them, but the photographs were intriguing. They saw the way their house used to look when it was new: bare unpainted wood on the outside, a barn beside it on the flat spot where the clothes-line now stood, an apple orchard on the hillside, and no trees obstructed the view of the lake from the house. Other photos showed the first residents, Mr. and Mrs. Charles Atkins, dressed all in black. She was wearing a high-collared black dress and large hat.

Lydia gasped, pointed and whispered, "That is her."

"That is who?" Isabelle asked.

"What? What are you talking about?" Anne chimed in.

Sarah said, "Let's all go home and we can talk about it there." They carefully closed the files and put them back in the file cabinet, then walked home.

Once seated at the table, Sarah encouraged Lydia to tell her story about the woman by her bed. Then immediately Anne told a story about hearing loud footsteps coming up the back steps to the second floor. But when she looked out in the hall, no one was there. She went to the kitchen and asked her mother if she had come upstairs and she said she had been right there in the kitchen the whole time. Sarah recalled the incident.

"What about you, Mum," Isabelle asked.

"I do have one story to tell, but your father might wish I did not tell you."

They all erupted at once swearing secrecy.

"Okay then. I will tell you about something curious that happened while we were moving in," she began. "Moving is exhausting and there were several boxes with non-essential items that were not unpacked right away. One evening as your father and I sat watching TV after you were all in bed, we heard a voice in the other room. We went to investigate and found the sound coming from one of the unpacked boxes. Inside was a transistor radio. At first we both brushed it off as a weird power surge and then immediately realized it was not plugged in, just running off a battery."

She watched their faces closely as they thought this over. "I feel very confident that there is nothing to be frightened of. Your father and I would never let harm come to any of you. I am sure they built this big house expecting to have children. Maybe it makes her happy to help look after you all. My personal belief is that there is much we don't under-stand and that is okay. But because your father believes only in science, that incident spooked him. So, don't talk about any of this, okay? And you can believe or not believe, as long as you are not scared. If you become scared then come to me and we will work it out together. Promise me."

They all promised, crossed their hearts and hoped to die, which Sarah told them was excessive. She believed. She wanted so much to know that there was a way between the now and the hereafter. One that was not frightening, but magical. She also wanted her children to experience the wonder of the unknown and to test their own imaginations. And growing up in this house in this beautiful place, what better way to enhance their memories than with a haunting? Sarah was well aware that the house was not really theirs to keep. It came with Bret's job and they were just renters. The children did not know the difference though. To them it was completely their own.

Bret's newest obsession was the restoration of a duck hunting boat. He found the frame in the woods along the lake and dragged it home. There he canvassed the exterior and painted it with a concoction of linseed oil and beeswax. Several trips down to the lake revealed leaks, but eventually it was watertight. He woke before dawn, launched it and paddled down to where Alamoosook turned into Dead River. It was marshy and overgrown with cattails and a good nesting spot for ducks and geese. He brought with him a string of wooden decoys his father had made years before. He brought home the beautifully feathered birds strung together by the feet. The sparse meat they provided was served as a treat, just a bite or two for each before dinner. After months of restoring the boat, this seemed a small reward, but Bret always had a project of some kind and his reward was always in the process of the project itself.

After shooting ducks a few times, he turned his spare energy into hand making a bow. This took several attempts, as he tested the strength and relative flexibility of different types of wood that he harvested from the forest. The final piece of art was made of maple with inlaid oak and hickory. He painted it with three coats of varnish, then set about making arrows to fit with store-bought metal points. He ventured out twice during bow hunting season, when the woods were free of over-eager, intoxicated rifle hunters from the city who were as likely to shoot each other as any deer. On his first outing, he tracked deer all day and missed a shot that went right between the legs of the doe. The next time he went out, he came home with a small doe and hung it in the garage. He and Sarah suffered through a long evening of trying to butcher it with no real knowledge of how to do it properly. This accomplished, he never hunted again, although the bow remained a prized possession.

With Anne now in school, Sarah chose a spring afternoon to talk with Bret about an interest she had. She asked him to go for a walk down by the lake. There was a fine mist in the air that felt refreshing. They found rocks to sit on near the lapping water's edge.

"I have been thinking a lot about what I should do with my time now that everyone is in school," she began. "I am thinking about going back to school."

"That is wonderful," Bret said. "What do you want to study?"

"I found a UMO catalog at the library. They have a nursing program. I thought that would be a really solid path for our future income," she told him.

"Yes, it would be. You know I am always supportive of education. But I honestly am surprised you never mentioned this before," he said.

"Well, it wasn't worth talking about until it could be possible. I wanted to get Anne settled in school and then see how I felt being home alone all day. I definitely need something productive to occupy my mind. And besides that, we need to think about the future. We have not even started down the road to home ownership. This would eventually enhance our income significantly."

He thought for a moment and then said, "Do you think we have made a mistake staying in a rented house?"

"No! Not at all. We all love this place and the house. We are living a dream raising those girls in that beautiful house. We will never be able to afford anything so grand. It is like living in a fairy tale."

"Would it be better to look for property we can buy to someday build on?"

"Yes, someday. But let me get a career going first."

"Then you should do it," he said and smiled at her.

"Okay. I am glad you agree," she smiled back at him. "But there is a cost. I think we would need to borrow money and I know you don't like debt."

"Look into it and we will go over the costs together and see what we can do."

"I will. And I also need to study for the entrance exam," she said. "I have been out of school for a long time – twenty-two years."

"Don't worry. You are smart. Nursing requires science courses. I can help you study for biology and chemistry tests."

They walked back home hand in hand both excited about something new in their lives.

That summer, the family took a camping trip to Baxter State Park. It was a beautiful drive there through winding roads in the dense forest. They selected a campsite with a wooden platform and lean-to roof. Inclement weather was a possibility and they were unsure if the canvas tent would hold up in a strong wind. It was starting to rip at the grommet holes from age and disuse. The camp cook stove was set up on the picnic table and Sarah made hamburgers for dinner.

The girls marched out into the woods repeatedly until they had a good pile of firewood. Their campfire burned late into the night. They star gazed and whittled sticks to roast marshmallows.

The next day, they visited one of the primary tourist attractions – the dump. Black bears came to the dump habitually and to accommodate the spectators, bleachers were erected by the park staff. They watched the bears for hours and could not help but feel sad for the bears rummaging through the debris.

The following day, they took a hike. Along the way, they saw a beautiful waterfall that came down onto a ledge before splashing further down the hillside. It seemed remote enough to Sarah that she ventured so far as to take off her T-shirt, then her shorts, and stand under the delightfully cold water while the others rested on nearby rocks. Then she looked up and much to her horror saw about a dozen people watching her from a fenced overlook above. She ran back to her family, dressed quickly and told them they needed to leave immediately. She was horribly embarrassed, but the unstoppable laughter from Bret and the kids soon helped her see the funny scene with less remorse.

They saw moose several times and lots of deer in the park. They returned home with bug bites, sunburns and the deep relaxation that comes from time spent outdoors.

Once back home, Bret raised the issue again of looking for property to buy.

"I know we aren't ready yet, but it would be fun to just look around and see what is available and for what price."

"Yeh, sure," Sarah said. "I can stop by the real estate office in town on Saturday and see what is listed."

That began a new activity of driving around on weekends past property for sale and dreaming about someday building a house.

One of the properties listed was just up the road a mile on Toddy Pond. The property was flat near the pond, offering a building site, and then continued up and over the top of a small mountainside. They walked along a fence line up through the woods until they reached a clearing at the top. They all sat in the sun to rest and look at the view. After a few minutes, Lydia stood up to stretch her legs and walked a short distance along the ridge.

"Hey," she called back. "I found something."

They all got up to investigate and found old dilapidated headstones half hidden in the underbrush and tall grass. One was so worn, no words could be seen. There was a rectangular depression where a coffin had collapsed beneath the earth, but no headstone nearby. Two of the headstones that sat side by side were clearly legible. One was two feet tall with a lamb engraved near the top, inscribed:

NELL CHANDLER OLSON
AND CHILD
1897

The other was just a few inches taller, and had a vine pattern around the curved top, inscribed:

EMILY ATKINS
BELOVED WIFE
1875 - 1904

"Why are they here, instead of in the cemetery?" Isabelle asked.

"People could be buried on private land back then," Bret answered. "I wonder if Emily was married to Charles Atkins who started the hatchery."

They spent a little more time looking around for more headstones, then concluded they had found everything to see. The sun was going down and they all headed down the mountain talking about what was planned for dinner, and trying to convince Sarah that dessert was warranted.

On the drive home, Bret pointed out an American Bald Eagle perched in a tall tree watching for fish below. Bret told them how important this was. They were an endangered species that had nearly become extinct. They were the national symbol and magnificent raptors. He pointed the bird out several times over the weeks ahead and made sure they watched for it and appreciated what they were seeing. These moments were precious to all of them, a shared experience of something ordinary made profound by experiencing it together.

All Hallows Eve

A S HALLOWEEN APPROACHED, THE girls were excited to dress up and go 'trick or treating.' There was much discussion about costumes and they all changed their minds several times before announcing to Sarah what they wanted to become on the night in question.

"I want to be a hobo," announced Isabelle.

"Okay. We can make that happen," Sarah said. "What about you?" she asked Lydia.

"I want to wear the wooden shoes in the playroom and have a Chinese woman's costume," Lydia said. The shoes had been found in a box of odds and ends purchased at an auction. Bret liked to get these boxes for next to nothing so the kids could discover the relics inside.

"And you?" she asked Anne.

"I want to be an owl," Anne said.

"An owl? Hmm. How can we make that?" Sarah asked.

"Cardboard wings and tail maybe?" Anne posed. She went in the sewing room, found some large pieces of construction paper, and started outlining wings with a pencil.

On the big day, Sarah bought a pumpkin at the Shop 'N Save and they all watched as Bret scooped out the inside and set them aside. Then he drew a face with all the girls making suggestions about the proper expression. They wanted it to be scary, but Bret said, "Let's not make it too scary." When they were all satisfied with the design, he carved the face, placed a candle inside, lit it with a match and turned off the lights. The girls were delighted.

While he was carving, Sarah had separated all the seeds from the pulp, rinsed them and tossed them in oil and salt to roast in the oven. She also made gingerbread cake, filling the house with the aromas of autumn spices.

Bret told them about the origins of the holiday going back to Celtic tradition of Samhain. Over time, the observance was merged with other fall traditions and became Halloween, he explained.

"Do you think the spirits come out on Halloween," Lydia asked.

"No, no. It is just a time for children to have fun. There is nothing to be afraid of," he said and looked at Sarah meaningfully.

She chimed in, but not in the way he had wanted, by saying, "Don't worry my little goblins, I will protect you." Bret rolled his eyes in exasperation.

There is something special about Halloween in New England. The Legend of Sleepy Hollow and Salem Witch Trials hang in the air between the old houses with wavy glass windows and the graveyards dating to the 1600s. Because the hatchery only had a few houses, trick or treating was done mostly from the car. Sarah drove them around looking for signs of those in the festive mood with jack-o-lanterns or other fall decorations displayed on the porches.

Unfortunately, it was bitter cold. Dark clouds scuttled quickly across the moon, creating images of witches on brooms in the children's imaginations. Sarah insisted they wear their coats for trick or treating, which caused much grumbling.

"How can they see our costumes?" Lydia complained.

"Okay, I get it. I will warm up the car. You can go without your coats. And likely catch pneumonia," she added under her breath. She drove them to various houses for treats. When they arrived at Ethel Snow's house, they were all invited to come in. Elderly Mrs. Snow admired their costumes and asked after each of them. Her traditional treats were Anne's favorite: buttery popcorn in little plastic sandwich bags.

After going house to house, Sarah dropped them off at a Halloween party at the Community Center, which used to be the grange hall. There they bobbed for apples, walked through a spook house in the back where adults dressed in costumes jumped out to scare them, and they were made to put their hands into a witches cauldron where hotdogs bumped into their hands as they were told they were dog turds, eliciting screams of horror.

They all marched around in a circle showing off their costumes, which were judged as to the most creative and the scariest in each age group. The prizes were caramel apples on sticks. When Sarah came to pick up the girls, they went home and dumped out their bags of candy on the living room floor, sorting and organizing the sickeningly sweet treasure trove.

"Make it last. Don't eat it all tonight," Sarah told them. They shared their treats with Bret and he declared he would only take those that were not their favorites. Because none of them had won the costume contest to receive a caramel apple, Lydia asked if they could make them sometime.

"Yes, of course," Sarah said. "The dentist is going to make a fortune from this family."

When it was time for bed and the lights were turned off upstairs, Anne pulled the covers up under her chin and thought about all the spirits out causing mischief. She was not at all sure she was safe in her bed. The wind blew the trees back and forth in the moonlight creating suspicious claw-like limbs across the wall above the bed. She lay awake for some time. Then Black and White cat jumped on her bed, which was very unusual. She curled up next to Anne's leg for warmth. Comforted, Anne finally fell into a deep sleep where she dreamed her costume wings were real and she flew about under the Halloween moon.

꧁꧂

After Jenny had left for Boston, Isabelle found a Ouija board left behind in the closet. It was just after Halloween, they decided to try and have a séance using the Ouiji board. Isabelle went down to the dining room chest of drawers to find candles and matches so they could properly set the stage for spirit interactions. They worked at it for a while without success.

Sarah, hearing none of the usual racket from upstairs came to check on them. She tiptoed down the hall. Finding no one in Lydia or Anne's rooms, she slowly turned the handle of the door going into Isabelle's room and opened it slowly with a creaking sound. There she found the girls sitting on the floor around the Ouiji board in the candlelight all staring at her wide-eyed, clearly expecting her to be a ghost.

"Watcha doin'?" Sarah asked suppressing a grin.

Isabelle's hand flew to her chest, "Mom! You scared us to death!"

"Any luck raising the dead this evening?" she teased.

"Not yet," Lydia sighed dramatically.

"Have fun," Sarah said and closed the door to go back downstairs.

The next day at school, Anne's second grade class was assigned to write a story about their family. Anne decided to write about their séance but did not know how to spell it. When she asked Miss Perkins how to spell the word, she received an odd look.

"What do you mean, Anne? What does the word mean you are looking to spell?"

"You know, when you light candles and try to conjure the spirits of the dead?" Anne explained.

"I am sure I don't know," said Miss Perkins, who then turned to look at her mother, Mrs. Perkins. Mrs. Perkins taught the fourth grade and often the two women visited each other's classrooms throughout the day.

Anne shrugged her shoulders and went back to her desk. She changed her sentence so she did not need to use words with mysterious spelling.

The next week, Miss Perkins asked Anne if she would like to go to dinner with her and her mother at a restaurant.

"Yes!" Anne replied excitedly.

"Ask your mother if we can pick you up tomorrow night at 5:30," Miss Perkins said.

When Anne asked Sarah, she said, "Yes, of course. How nice of them. It is rather unusual. What do you think brought this on?"

Anne thought for a minute and then said, "I did ask them how to spell séance and they both looked a little shocked. I wrote my paper about it. Maybe they think I need to be saved from a wicked home life," she speculated.

Sarah started to laugh, and said, "You are probably, right."

Bret heard all this and was concerned. "Good grief, Sarah. They will be coming after us with torches soon. You have to remember we are in a very traditional, rural place."

Sarah could not stop laughing.

Beggars Would Ride

C HARLES CAME IN THE tavern occasionally and greeted Emily warmly. She assumed he was especially friendly because she was Nell's best friend. However, she could not help but be attracted to him and her flirtations were reciprocated. Her parents observed this and questioned her.

"I thought he was courting your friend Nell," her father, Peter, asked.

"He is," she said as she smiled wistfully watching him leave the tavern.

"Then what are you doin' flirting like that?" asked her mother, Hannah.

"He seems to like it when I flirt with him. Who says he is going to marry Nell? Maybe he will change his mind and ask me out," Emily said as if in jest.

Hannah laughed. "Well, I can't say I blame you, girl. If I was younger..."

"Hey now!" Peter interjected. "That is enough of that."

"Hannah patted him on the cheek and said, "Now, now, old man. Nothin' for you to worry about. I'm yours to keep."

Emily did not tell Nell about Charles coming in the tavern or about any of their flirtatious conversations. But she did keep asking for all the details Nell knew about him. She was studying the situation and wondering if she might get a chance at him eventually.

Emily was in the full bloom of her newfound womanhood and was pining for some romance of her own. With no other reasonable prospects in town, she started tracking Charles habits and his routes through town and found numerous times to accidently run into him. She was clever and creative in her comments to him and he never failed to respond in kind.

Hannah observed all this and teased Emily about her feelings for Charles. Hannah naturally wanted the very best for her daughter and thought Emily had every right to try to attract the attention of the handsome newcomer. She would sit on the edge of Emily's bed at night and ask questions about Emily's interactions with Charles. She could see the spark in her daughter's eye and felt the rush of young love vicariously.

After a few months had passed, Hannah decided to give the situation a nudge. She called Emily into her room and took a small cloth bag out of the back of her dresser drawer. They sat side by side on the bed.

"Emily, dear, I have something special I want to give you. This is something that has been in my family for a very long time, passed down through the generations." And she pulled out a piece of polished amethyst about an inch in diameter with a silver rim.

Emily's eyes grew big and she said, "Oh, mother. That is beautiful! I can't believe you have never showed it to me before."

"Well, it is something very special and I only pass it to you now because you are old enough to use it wisely."

"Use it. Whatever do you mean?" Emily asked, confused.

"This is an amulet. Do you know what that is?" she asked

"No," Emily admitted.

"It is a type of charm. It has been imbued with a spell to help the owner through life. Do you understand? It can increase your luck, you could say. But, listen carefully. It is not to be misused. You must use it for good. Do you understand?"

"Yes, Mom. Why are you giving it to me now?"

Hannah gave a crooked smile, "Let's just say love is one of its many possible uses."

Emily smiled at her mother. "You are a bit wicked, mother."

"Not at all," Hannah said, feigning offense. "It is simply your time to have this precious item."

❦

ONE DAY WHEN NELL was taking noon dinner to her father at the post office, she saw Charles and Emily coming out of the tavern arm in arm and walking ahead of her down the street. She stopped in her tracks and watched them. Emily was swinging her hips seductively, smiling, and laughing up into his face. He was reciprocating in kind. Her cheeks started to burn. When she dropped off her father's meal, he took one look at her and said, "Alright, dear?"

"Just not feeling well today, Dad. I will be alright," she mumbled dismissively. She hurried home deep in thought.

The incident bothered her, but she soon forgot it as her time with Charles went on inspiring dreams of future marital bliss. Jealousy was a bad trait she did not wish to own. But as the months went on and Charles poured his energy into his project, she began to feel less and less sure things were going her way. She did not speak to her mother or Emily about this, but doubts were beginning to take up a lot of her thoughts.

As winter set in, the nature of their outings turned to sleigh rides and hot drinks by the fire at the Inn afterwards. On one of these occasions, Charles surprised Nell by inviting Emily along.

He greeted her at her door as usual, then as they walked out to the sleigh he said, "I invited your friend Emily to join us. I was sure you would not mind." He smiled at her warmly as he helped her into the sleigh borrowed from the livery stable owner. "There is a small party gathering out on the Orland River tonight."

Nell smiled at him, but hesitated. Then she said, "Oh. Well, of course!" with false enthusiasm. She felt his decision to invite Emily was inconsiderate. But she loved Emily and always had a wonderful time when she was around. As she tried to sort out these feelings, they pulled up in front of the Jenkins house and saw Emily watching out the window. She hurried out the door and ran down the walk to the sleigh sliding playfully on her boots the last three feet. She was all bundled in her warmest coat, scarf, hat and hand muffler. She looked exuberant and charming.

Charles reached out and pulled Emily up into the seat beside him on the opposite side of Nell and they set off. It was a splendidly cold night and the stars were bright, illuminating the landscape with only the help of a small crescent moon. They swooshed through the snow at a steady trot and chatted about idle things like the brilliant stars, constellations they knew, and the way the cold made their eyes blur with tears. Nell worked hard to keep her mood steady and stay engaged in the conversation.

As they approached the river, they saw a bonfire lit at the frozen water's edge, down the hill from the Congregational Church. There were about a dozen merry makers standing around the fire, singing bawdy songs, and sipping beverages from shared cups passed between them. The truth was that Nell's parents probably would not like her associating with this rowdy crowd from the tavern. However, she was escorted by Charles and they thought he was beyond reproach.

They climbed down from the sleigh and were welcomed by the jolly crowd. The fire was a reprieve from the cold and soon they were so warm they had to step back from the fire. As Nell stood close by Charles, she was suddenly hit from behind with a snowball. They both turned to discover that Emily was the culprit. Charles immediately packed a snowball between his leather gloves and threw it at her as she ran away. Others joined in the fun, and a skirmish ensued for the next five minutes, during which Nell stood stoically gazing into the fire.

When everyone settled back down, Charles pointed to the sky and said, "Look!" Everyone turned their heads and silence ensued as they watched a long shimmering ribbon of green slide gracefully across the sky with a halo of gold along the top edge. The northern lights were painting the sky with swimming electro-magnetic energy in hues of blue, green, gold and white. It was magical and brought a much-needed joy to Nell's troubled mood. She reached over for Charles hand and he smiled at her and squeezed her hand warmly.

They stayed for about an hour in all. The ride home was mostly quiet. When they dropped off Emily, she thanked Charles and said, "See you tomorrow," to Nell. Nell nodded her head. When Charles stopped at her house, she hopped down quickly saying a brief goodnight over her shoulder and saw herself to the door.

That night she lay in her bed thinking. Was something going wrong, or was everything okay? She did not have any experience to compare it to. Maybe Charles was genuinely trying to please her by including Emily in their lives together. And, she loved Emily so much. They were like sisters. But there was a feeling of unease that was creeping into her bones. When she finally fell into a restless sleep, she dreamed of a peaceful place where a waterfall splashed into a green pool surrounded by lush vegetation. She sat at the water's edge and looked up into the sky. A raven flew low over the pool and dropped something into the pool right at her feet. She looked down to find it was a dead baby bird. She tried to scream, but no sound came out, and she woke with a gasp.

I N FEBRUARY, HE SEEMED especially distracted and they had not seen each other for three weeks. He came by the house and asked if she would have dinner with him at the Inn on Friday. She immediately felt silly about her doubts. She dressed carefully, put her hair up, wore dangling earrings, and powdered her face. He was as debonair as ever. After she decided to have lamb, he placed the order for her and the same for himself. He talked animatedly about his work since he last saw her and she tried to be attentive. But the longer he talked, the more she drifted into her thoughts about doubting his intentions.

"Are you feeling quite alright, Nell," he asked. "You seem distracted."

"Oh, I am fine," she said. "Perhaps a little tired is all."

"I understand. We can make an early night of it, if you like," he said.

They ate with little conversation, and he walked her up the hill to her house. He kissed her hand as he always had and bid her goodnight. She went in and closed the door quietly so as not to alert her parents she was home, waited a minute, then went back out and followed him at a distance. He went to the tavern. She could see from across the street him sitting at the bar and Emily leaning over the bar smiling and talking with him. Tears stung her eyes. She went home with her heart pounding wondering what she should do.

Charles called on her after that but less frequently, perhaps every few weeks. They had less fun together than before because Nell was remote and mistrustful. Emily continued to ask her all about what they did together, but Nell offered less and less information.

"What is wrong? I am your best friend. Why aren't you telling me about Charles anymore," Emily implored. Nell shrugged her shoulder and declined to answer. She found excuses to spend less and less time with Emily. Even when she missed her friend, she would recall the sight of Charles with Emily and feel betrayed and bereft. It was infuriating in so many ways.

Then her mother told her that she heard gossip about Charles taking Emily to Bangor to buy supplies. After that, he stopped calling on her. Nell was so depressed that she rarely went out. Her parents were deeply concerned for her.

Nell spent the summer isolating herself. She stayed home or went out walking in the country alone. When her mother asked her to do errands in town, she made excuses. Her mother understood and stopped asking.

In the fall, Charles and Emily announced their engagement to everyone at the tavern. News spread quickly, Maynard told his wife, and then they both went to tell Nell. She wept uncontrollably. It was unthinkable that her best friend for so many years would do this. And what had Charles been thinking leading her on like that? Were they both simply cruel, or does love blind people to others around them?

Nell stewed in her painful wrath for two months. Then she decided she missed both of them too much to throw away any chance of friendship. If she did not make up with Emily, she might die of loneliness in this town. She went to Emily, apologized for her jealousy, and wished her congratulations on her engagement. She swallowed her pride and worked with Emily on designing and sewing a wedding dress and was her maid of honor at the wedding held at the Congregational Church. A reception at the tavern went on late into the night, hosted by the parents of the bride.

Though Maynard and Geneva were invited, they declined to attend and wondered at their daughter's fortitude. But the truth was that, despite herself, Nell was not all right. She was all wrong, filled with betrayal and thoughts of revenge.

Box of Letters

1967: MRS. WHITE TAUGHT first grade. She was elderly, white-haired, soft-spoken, and gentle. The children loved her. She not only taught first graders, but also taught adults how to be good parents to first graders. She called and asked Sarah to practice reading with Anne every evening. Within no time, it all started to make sense and Anne's confidence grew more.

The next time, Mrs. White called to tell Sarah that Anne was excelling wonderfully with her reading. Sarah and Bret were so pleased. However, she also wanted to talk about something else.

"Perhaps Anne told you that I used to live in the big hatchery house with my husband Clayton. He ran the hatchery in the forties and fifties and we lived there for 22 years," Mrs. White told her.

"Oh, yes, she did tell me," Sarah said.

"I just loved that house and the yard and the big trees there when they turn in the fall. So majestic," Mrs. White reminisced.

"We love it here, too. We feel so lucky to get to live in this house," Sarah said.

"Well, I thought you might be interested in something I have. When we moved in, we had to clear out some boxes left in the attic. Behind stacks of newspapers and boxes of old clothes, we found a small box of letters. They are letters received by the first lady of the house when it was built. From a sister or a cousin maybe," Mrs. White said.

"How marvelous," Sarah said, intrigued.

"Of course we told the people at the regional office about them in case they wanted to archive them, but they said that personal letters were not of interest to them for archiving. I didn't have the heart to throw them out and so I still have them. I thought perhaps you would find them interesting," she said.

"Yes, of course! I would love to read them. My girls would like that too. They are very interested in the history of the house," Sarah said.

"Come by my house on Back Ridge Road any time after 4:00 p.m. That is when I get home from the school. I will have them ready."

"Thank you so much for thinking of us. I can't wait to see them!"

Sarah hung up the phone feeling excited and wondering if they might get some good clues about the Atkins Family.

The very next day, Sarah stopped by Mrs. White's house at 4:30 in the afternoon. It was a large two-story gabled roof house, likely built around the same time as the hatchery house. Mrs. White met her at the door with the small cardboard box, about the size of a shoebox. It smelled musty just like the attic it had been in for so many years. She thanked Mrs. White and promised to return them.

"Oh, no. You keep them," Mrs. White said. "I have always felt like they shouldn't be in my hands, but didn't know what to do with them. Maybe they belong to the house," she suggested.

"Maybe. Thank you, again," she called as she walked back to the car. She drove the mile and half home and immediately put the box away until dinner was ready and everyone had been fed. Then as the girls washed the dishes, she slipped upstairs to preview the letters. She wanted to share them with the girls, but wanted to have an idea of their contents first. Every one of them, perhaps twenty in all, were addressed to Mrs. Charles Atkins, East Orland, ME 04431. The return address in the upper left corner was Mrs. Riley, Nashua, NH.

Sarah took a few out of their envelopes and saw the letters were to "My Dear Emily," and signed "Truly yours, Bridget." She could be a sister, cousin, or old school friend. It was impossible to know unless the letters revealed something. The grave they found was undoubtedly this Emily. The content seemed to be general news and replies to Emily's letters. She put them away and decided she would read them aloud to the girls, a few each night before bedtime. That evening at eight o'clock, she herded the girls up to start getting ready for bed.

She checked on Bret to ensure he was entertained for a bit. He was deep in his newest obsession making wooden kitchen utensils. He sat in his chair in front of the television with a plywood sheet resting on the chair arms to create a worktable. He had already made three different sizes of long handled spoons, two slotted spoons, and a ladle. Now he was making a mallet for tenderizing meat. One side of the head was carved into rows of grooved edges, the other side was in a diamond-hatched pattern. He was utterly lost in his craft, using fine detailing tools.

Sarah went upstairs and found the girls in their nightgowns with teeth brushed. They gathered in Isabelle's room and sat on the bed. Sarah opened the first letter, having arranged them carefully in date order. She read aloud.

April 21, 1892

My Dear Emily,

I was so delighted to receive your letter! Congratulations on your engagement! Mr. Atkins sounds wonderful according to your account. If it was possible for me to come to your wedding, you know I would be there. Roger is very busy at the millworks and cannot get away. He is in line for a possible promotion to operations supervisor over the shift foremen. There is no way he would allow me to travel alone all that way unescorted, so I have not even asked him. But I did tell him about your betrothal and he sends his best wishes.

I can hardly believe it has been over three years since I saw you. I think about you all the time and imagine what a beautiful young lady you have become. Let me know when you find out where you will be living and please keep writing to me. Bless Johanna for giving you my new address here. We must not lose touch again.

I assume your parents are doing fine or you would have told me otherwise. Please send my regards to them both.

Yours truly,

Bridget

As she refolded it and put it in the envelope, she asked the girls, "What do you think their relationship is? She can't be a sister or they would not have lost touch."

"But Bridget does know Emily's parents," Isabelle offered.

"Maybe Bridget is her aunt," Lydia offered.

"If she is getting married, she must be twenty-one at least," Anne said.

"Not necessarily," Sarah said. "Girls got married younger back then. She may only be sixteen, or even younger."

"What? Getting married while in High School?" Isabelle asked.

"A lot of people, especially girls, did not go to school after eighth grade back then," Sarah said. "But don't get any ideas. You are all going to high school and then college." She looked at each of them in turn.

"Well, let's read another and see if we get any more clues," Sarah said. "This next one is almost a year later."

December 15, 1892

My Dear Emily,

Your holiday greeting letter arrived just today and I could not wait to reply. You sound positively in love. It is wonderful that Nell helped make the wedding special. I am not surprised the two of you are still so close.

Your home, festooned with holiday balsam garlands sounds lovely and so fragrant. I am so happy for you. I suppose you will be expecting a little one soon and I want to know right away.

Little William is just now giving up nursing, so I expect I may be becoming pregnant again soon. My best advice to you is to find the very best midwife. They are not all the same! My friend here had a horrible time delivering and swears that the midwife was useless. She neither comforted her nor helped her. Luckily, all went well in the end.

I think I told you that Roger was hoping for a promotion. He got it in July and is so much happier. He no longer has to spend any time on the milling floor where the fabric lint was ruining his lungs. He is up in the office and can sit near an open window when the weather allows.

The project Charles is working on sounds so interesting. And all the time you are spending out at the lake is good for your health. Write to me again soon.

Yours truly,

Bridget

"They must be about the same age to both be talking about having babies," Isabelle said. "And Nell is the other grave on the mountain."

"What is the milling floor," Anne asked.

"Sounds like Roger works in a textile mill. That is why the fabric lint was bad for his lungs. That area was big in textile manufacturing," Sarah said. "Okay, girls. Time for lights out. School tomorrow."

"Can we read more tomorrow?" Lydia asked. "And can it be in my room next?"

"Yes, of course," Sarah said and kissed them all goodnight in their own beds and turned out the lights.

As she was doing this, Anne said, "I am going to college to be a veterinarian."

Isabelle said, "I am going to be a lawyer."

Lydia said, "I am going to be a stuntman in Hollywood."

"Terrific. Now go to sleep," Sarah said and turned off the hall light. She went downstairs to join Bret in the living room.

"What are you girls up to?" he asked.

"Anne's teacher, Mrs. White used to live here in this house. She had letters written to the first lady of the house, Emily Atkins. She passed them on to me and I am reading them to the girls," she said.

"How fun. Are they interesting?" he asked.

"Yes, I think the girls are actually getting interested in history by imagining these people in the letters," she said.

"That is great. Let me know if you learn anything about the hatchery itself. I would be interested," he said.

"Sure, but so far it is just personal conversations between two women. You know. Girl stuff. Which is why it is so fascinating to the kids," she said and smiled at him, knowing he would understand that it was not really his sort of thing.

Each evening they read two letters, so they lasted ten days. Most of the letters were about everyday things and family life. Bridget had a little girl in 1893, and then she wrote to Emily consoling her in October 1894 when Emily had a miscarriage.

October 1894
My Dear Emily,

My heart breaks for you. I am so sorry for your loss. To lose a baby at only a few months can be difficult enough, but to lose your child at five months is dreadful. I wish I were there to wrap my arms around you. I will pray for your baby's soul and for your heart to heal. I know this must be devastating for Charles as well. Tell him he is in my thoughts.

Please don't let this tragedy make you give up. I feel sure you will have more chances for the blessing of children in your life. I know you take the best care of your health, but maybe the midwife can provide you with extra tinctures to help promote a healthy full-term pregnancy. Ask her at least.

Stay focused on what is positive to keep your spirits up. The house plans for the hatchery are a good place to start. You can be an influence in making it the house of your dreams. Tell Charles what you want and like and he can work with the architect to make it perfect for you.

Never give up hope in the future.

Yours truly,

Bridget

This upset the girls, and also piqued their interest to ask many questions. Sarah took the opportunity to tell them all about having children and how it was more dangerous in the olden days without modern medicine. Then a letter revealed that the house was finished and Charles and Emily moved in. The girls listened with rapt attention as they envisioned Emily and Charles in the very room where they were reading the letter, which was Sarah's room this time.

April 5, 1897

My Dear Emily,

How exciting that you will be in the new house within a month! I am so happy that you insisted on four bedrooms upstairs so there will be plenty of room for your family. Your wallpaper selections sound beautiful. I love that you chose different colors and patterns for each room.

Planning to have Nell's wedding there is perfect. I wish I could be there to see her father escorting her down the grand front stairs. You are such a good friend to her. Please tell her I wish her and Michael the very best in their future together.

I am still waiting to hear good news from you about "you know what." Tell Charles he isn't trying hard enough. Only joking, don't really tell him that. I am knitting a layette for you in yellow for either a girl or a boy. I will send it in a few weeks.

Yours truly,
Bridget

The next letter had bad news that Sarah read to the girls.

December 5, 1897
My Dear Emily,

I am weeping as I write this. I am shocked at your misfortune and unable to adequately express my dismay. Again, I wish I were there with you. I am so glad Nell is at your side. There must be some explanation of why you are not carrying these children to full term. Losing children in the second trimester is so unusual.

Please know that you did nothing wrong. I know you took care of yourself during your pregnancy and I know Charles would not let you do anything dangerous to the baby. I can only imagine the little graveyard you have started up the hill from your new home. Two little headstones, side by side. A testament to the cruelty of nature.

You are in my thoughts and prayers. I am with you in this great time of grief.

Yours truly,

Bridget

"Mum. That is why she is still here. That is why she looks over us," Lydia said to Sarah wide-eyed. "She could not have any kids to fill this big house that they designed with three children's rooms."

"That is a very good theory. It sounds like she was having a terrible time trying to have children," Sarah replied.

"That is why she isn't scary. She just wants to be a mother in a house full of kids," Anne said.

They all sat quietly for a while deep in thought about Emily, Charles, Bridget, and Nell. They were long gone and yet so close in that house. It was compelling and they all longed to know more.

"I wonder if we can find the graves of the babies," Isabelle asked.

"We might be able to. It is all overgrown, but if we find the highest part of the rise behind the house, maybe we can find something," Sarah said. They all went to bed eager for the weekend when they could undertake the expedition to find the graves of Emily's tragic children.

The next night was Thursday and they read more letters. The most interesting left more questions than answers.

August 4. 1898

My Dear Emily,

I have been speechless for four days trying to decide how to respond. Your news is disturbing in several ways. Nell was your best friend. The death of her and her baby is so sad. It sounds like neither one had a chance after she lost too much blood. There is only so much a midwife can do. I also feel sorry for her husband. They were barely through their first year of marriage, a bond that should have lasted a lifetime.

But, the theft is so very troubling. How could she steal from you? Especially something so precious and valuable as a family heirloom. The other part about your suspicions of misuse of the charm, I don't have words. That sounds like an unholy power, and one that you acknowledge could have been used for harm. Why on earth would Nell want to harm anyone?

Please write back soon. Your letters mean so much to me.

Yours truly,

Bridget

The girls all stared at Sarah wide-eyed. "So sad that Nell died in childbirth," Sarah said.

"Does the baby always die, too," Anne asked.

"No, sometimes the baby survives even if the mother doesn't. But usually they both die," Sarah said. "When a baby is in a woman's womb they are deeply connected. They share blood and antibodies. Any trauma to the mother is shared with the baby. It is like they are one thing until the umbilical cord is cut."

Anne reached over deep in thought and placed her hand on Sarah's abdomen. Sarah smiled, "And they are connected afterwards, too, in different ways. All five of you will always be a part of me."

"What about this mysterious charm?" Isabelle asked. "It sounds evil."

"Yes, that is very intriguing. I need to think about it," Sarah said. "And it is late now. Let's all sleep on it and talk tomorrow." She tucked them in and turned out their lights."

"Mum?" Lydia said.

"What, baby girl?"

"Do you believe in evil," Lydia asked.

Sarah took a deep breath. "I think people make bad choices sometimes. But evil does not exist on its own. Now sleep and don't worry, okay?"

"Okay. Love you, Mum."

"Love you more," Sarah said.

When Saturday rolled around, everyone was up early ready to go explore in the woods for headstones. Sarah made the girls wait until she had stuffed them with quiche fresh out of the oven. She told Bret what they were up to and he was hesitant.

"Really? They want to go searching for the graves of two babies? Don't they find any of this scary?" Bret asked.

"They are totally excited. It is like playing detective. Want to come along?" Sarah asked.

"No. You all have a good time. My ankle is throbbing with the change in weather and I don't need a hike in the woods today."

"Okay. Suit yourself," and she set a plate of quiche, sausages and toast on his lap and kissed his bald head.

They set off up the road to the nature trail and then when the ground started to dip back down, they veered to the left, which would be the area above the old orchard. It was windy and clouds raced across the sky and whooshed through the tree branches above. The woods were thick and they picked their way around downed trees and thickets trying to stay on the highest ground. They meandered back and forth looking and digging their toes in the ground where they found small mounds. The ground was thick and squishy with many layers of dead leaves, pine needles, and bark. They examined mushrooms in a rotten log and talked about how quickly nature decomposes wood.

"If the headstones were wooden, they could be long gone," Sarah told them.

"What else do they make headstones from?" Lydia asked.

"Oh, they can be made of stone, cement, or metal. Those materials still weather but much more slowly. Remember how hard it was to read some of the headstones we found on the mountain above Toddy Pond? Those were made of cement, but very old." Sarah said.

After an hour, they decided the headstones must have been made of wood and were no longer there. They traipsed back to the house, each thinking their own thoughts about how fleeting our time on earth is before everyone just turns to dust.

"Do you think the bones of the babies are still down there under the ground," Anne asked.

"That depends on what sort of casket they were put in. It was probably wood, which would have deteriorated even faster than the headstones since they were underground. Then the bones would deteriorate, too." Sarah said.

⁓

N O MATTER WHAT THE weather, the teachers insisted that the children spend recess outside to burn off energy and clear their heads. Recess was the place where socializing occurred. Friends were made, common interests were discovered, and popularity played itself out to the pain and embarrassment of many.

Sarah said that boys teased girls because they liked them. Depending on the type of teasing, it was apparent to Anne that this was not always the motivation. The boys who dangled giant night crawlers into their mouths and swallowed them on the playground for attention were definitely wasting their time. The girls were unimpressed. There were a few of these same boys whose favorite recess activity was drawing unflattering pictures in the dirt with sticks and naming them after the girls. The girls in turn spent much time scuffing the images away with their feet.

One day Anne decided she had had enough and decided it was time to do something to restore order among the tribe. She methodically approached every group of children on the playground, which included all the kindergarten through second graders – about 70 children. She said, "Let's 'get' those boys." She had not really thought through what might happen, but received an almost unanimous expression of support from her classmates. Within minutes everyone had chased the three offending boys into a corner of the building and began hitting and kicking them. Anne stood back in dismay at this horrifying sight, which luckily was quickly diffused by Mrs. Heath, the teacher on playground duty. When she asked what on earth everyone thought they were doing, they all pointed at Anne and said she told them to do it.

Mrs. Heath stared at Anne in disbelief. Anne was speechless. She received neither punishment nor reprimand. Maybe Mrs. Heath knew by the look on Anne's face that she was equally surprised. The boys received bloody noses, bruised shins, and deeply wounded pride. Anne did not feel she had won anything, except a new respect for the burden of leadership. She could not quite understand how a suggestion could cause a riot. Each child must have felt the same rage toward those boys, but had no way to express or resolve it. Anne did not tell her parents and, apparently, her sisters did not hear about it at school.

When the next school year rolled around, Anne was placed in the highest reading group in the second grade. Later that year, her teacher asked her to transcribe the lessons from notes to the chalkboard when she arrived in the morning on the early bus. She was friends with everyone and starting to really like school.

Three girls in Anne's class liked to sing and the teacher encouraged them by letting them stand up and sing to the class. The two songs they knew were popular on the radio and totally inappropriate for second graders. They were *Divorce* by Tammy Wynette and *Harper Valley PTA* by Jeannie C. Riley. Anne figured the PTA part maybe appealed to the teacher.

By 1968, all three of the girls had long hair as was the fashion. But they were not so good at taking care of it and Sarah grew tired of struggling with them to get it untangled. That summer she gave up and left them to their own devices. Isabelle was old enough to keep things in order, but Lydia and Anne's hair became a ridiculous matted mess. As school approached, Sarah announced that their hair would need to be cut. This was considered an unacceptable infringement on their personal style and they decided they should run away in rebellion. Isabelle helped by escorting them up the lane to the nature trail that meandered through the woods. After much talk about how they could never go back, Isabelle said she would go get provisions.

She entered the door nearest the kitchen and walked stealthily. Sarah was nowhere to be seen. She grabbed a sleeve of crackers, a jar of Marshmallow Fluff, and a butter knife. She checked to make sure no one was watching her and then ran up the trail to find her sisters at the hideout. They spent the afternoon gorging themselves on the sticky snacks. When the air began to cool, they decided they would have to go back. They planned a speech in which Sarah would be made to understand the importance of their hair. They also considered if it would be possible to get the tangles out.

They slipped back into the house unnoticed and went upstairs to Isabelle's room. There they set to work with all the hair potions and devices they could find to try to solve the problem. Eventually with sore heads and a good amount of pulled-out hair on the floor, they declared the tangles gone. They went to find Sarah who was making dinner in the kitchen. She appeared unfazed by their absence most of the day.

"Look Mum," Lydia said and turned around swinging her black locks from side to side. Anne followed suit and did the same.

"Good," Sarah said. "Keep it that way." It had been a very narrow escape, and Lydia and Anne worked hard to make sure it never happened again.

That evening after dinner, Bret called the girls down from upstairs to show them something. They all walked slowly and quietly down the fire lane where they heard a Great Horned Owl hooting. Bret passed around the binoculars and pointed at where to look. Then suddenly, the owl launched silently from its branch high in the trees and swooped low right over their heads without a sound. It was magical. Bret told them on the way back to the house that they have special feathers that make their flight silent to their prey.

Keep Enemies Close

NELL DREAMED AT NIGHT of living in the big proposed house with Charles. She dreamed that he loved her and they were incredibly happy. Then she would wake and remember the truth. Her heart would pound and she would feel ill. It was hard to believe and harder to accept.

Nell should have distanced herself from Charles and Emily, but instead she immersed herself in their lives. After the wedding, Charles rented a house for himself and Emily in East Orland near the post office. The house was a tiny structure built fifty years earlier. It had a small front room, and back kitchen, and stairs up to one bedroom. A shed addition off the kitchen had a bathroom added the year before. Charles assured his bride it was only temporary as he continued to negotiate with the federal government about partnering with him on the hatchery development. The dream house was going to become a reality at the government's expense; it was just a matter of time.

Through years of letters back and forth and many official visits, Charles did attract funding for his project from the US Department of the Interior, who eventually purchased the land. The large house would overlook the lake and double as a hatchery office. Charles and Emily, often with Nell in tow, visited the construction site daily watching artisans craft the house as designed by a Department of the Interior architect.

At the exorbitant cost of $5,000, the design included custom woodwork on the mantles, doors and banisters. The wood flooring was milled in New York and brought by train. The barn with four stalls and a hayloft was built concurrently. Charles planted an apple orchard on the hill above the house. Much of the land had been logged years before leaving a clear view of the lake. He planted three trees, an oak, a maple, and an elm, in what would become a yard with a circular drive.

Charles treated Nell with kind affection. He smiled warmly, and always thanked her for her devotion to his wife. Sometimes Nell would go home to her parents' house wondering if she had imagined the whole thing between them. She had fallen in love, but maybe for him, it was just a companionable friendship from the beginning. She was dying to know the details of their intimate life, but Emily never revealed anything and Nell refused to ask.

Nell was at their house often. She came bearing baskets of baked goods or fresh-cut flowers and spent time with Emily. When Charles was with them she disguised her affection for him as well as her animosity toward him, for her emotions were a complex tangle of desire and scorn.

Emily confided her concern that she had not conceived and talked with Nell about it often. Nell secretly hoped she never would. Emily having Charles' child filled her with rage she could barely handle. On a trip to Bangor with her parents, Nell said she would meet up with them later and ventured off to shop alone.

Following a route told to her by a crone in the city park, she made her way down an alley to a red door with Chinese symbols painted on it in black. She knocked and was greeted wordlessly by a solemn Chinese woman dressed in oversized loose men's pants and a long tunic. The woman looked up and down the alley.

Seeing no one, she gestured for Nell to enter and closed the door.

The exotic aroma of herbs hanging from racks attached to the ceiling filled the air of the close, dusty room. Bottles and jars lined floor-to-ceiling shelves on all the walls, each with a paper label tied around the bottleneck showing Chinese characters.

The woman stared at her, unmoving and not speaking. Nell hesitated, then spoke, hoping she would be understood.

"I wish to end an accidental pregnancy," Nell said, placing her hands over her abdomen.

The woman nodded. She walked to a ladder and climbed to a top shelf, taking down a jar of dried herbs. She placed a spoonful of the herbs into a small vial filled with liquid and put a cork stopper in the top. The woman put out her hand palm up to Nell. Nell searched in her pocket, pulled out a coin, and placed it in her hand. The woman looked at the coin and held her hand back out. Nell placed another coin in her hand and the woman did not move, so she placed another, and the woman nodded and went behind the counter.

She gave Nell a dropper, and held up four fingers. Then she pointed to the calendar and pointed one after another for ten days. Nell hoped she understood correctly, four drops per day for ten days.

Knowing that Emily had trouble conceiving and that many pregnancies were lost in the early months, she waited to see what would happen. She hid her disgust at Emily's and Charles' excitement over the pregnancy. Nell and Emily's parents were the only ones who knew early on, but when she started to show, everyone was so happy for the young couple. Laurel's mother organized a baby shower for Emily and many women and girls from Bucksport, Orland, and East Orland attended the event in the park in Bucksport.

Emily was hoping for a large family and kept encouraging Charles to tell the architect they needed at least three children's rooms in the new house that was to be built. Nell found excuses to come to their house nearly every day that October. This was unusual, but she was greeted with open arms as usual. She told Emily to keep her feet up and made her lunch and brought beverages dosed with the tincture droplets.

After a few weeks, Emily began to feel ill. Nell arrived to find her pale and suffering from abdominal pains. These increased until Charles sent for the midwife. Of course, it was much too early for the baby to come. The midwife could do nothing, but was there to confirm the news when the child was aborted in a bloody congealed mass. The head and tiny hands and feet were formed. She wrapped the mess inside a blanket and left the couple to mourn. Nell came back the next day and went with them to the hill above where the new house would be built. Charles dug a small grave and they placed the bundle in the ground with prayers for the soul of the unbaptized child.

Over the next week, Charles borrowed chisels and carved a headstone from a piece of maple board. It read "Our Beloved Child, Taken in 1894."

Nell felt nothing. She did not care about their grief, as they had not cared about hers.

Emily and Charles considered Nell their dearest friend, always there for them. As time wore on, they were concerned that she was approaching twenty-two years old and was unmarried. When a new postmaster came to East Orland, Nell's father, Maynard, was assigned to train him in his new position. Michael Olson was twenty-four and had moved there from Searsport. He was a kind person, of average looks and build. He was very friendly and had a keen interest in the neighbors he met in East Orland. He told Maynard he hoped to marry and start a family of his own there. Maynard and Geneva invited him to supper at their home and hoped that he and Nell might strike up a romance.

Michael saw Nell often, since she visited Charles and Emily on a regular basis. He would walk out on the porch, wave to her, and holler hello. Then he began crossing the street to talk with her when she was about. Finally, he worked up his nerve and asked if she might accompany him down to the fish hatchery to see the new house under construction. Nell saw this as another opportunity to further spy on Charles and gladly accepted.

Emily and Charles thought this was a good sign and encouraged both Michael and Nell in their friendship. Michael found Nell quite fetching. As for Nell, she found him better than no one. He provided company and conversation. He was kind and considerate. And, as Maynard and Geneva told her repeatedly, he had a good career that could support a family. When he asked for her hand in marriage, she literally shrugged her shoulders and said, "Why not?"

This was not the acceptance Michael had envisioned, but he figured she would come around once they settled into married life. Emily and Charles insisted she get married at their new beautiful house on the lake, which both Nell and Michael thought a very generous offer. Emily and Nell began making plans right away with invitation lists, dress pattern designing, fabric shopping, and finding a caterer. For this was going to be a grand event and would also be a sort of housewarming.

Two weeks after the engagement was made, Emily announced she believed she was pregnant again. With tears in her eyes, she and Charles shared a glass of sherry with Nell and Michael to celebrate both the impending wedding and the much-anticipated child. Despite Maynard's and Geneva's doubts whether it was good for Nell to continue her close relationship with Charles and Emily, they reluctantly had to conclude that it was beyond their influence. They thought the wedding at the new house would be a lovely and memorable event and hoped it would make Nell happy.

The day of the event fell three months after Charles and Emily had moved in and decorated their new home. Nell worked side by side with Emily planting a rose and lilac garden in the back yard, and a bed of peonies, daisies, and lavender in the front yard.

Carriages carrying wedding guests began arriving at noon on a beautiful clear, sunny, windless day. Tables had been brought and set out on the lawn to extend the reception area on the wide front porch overlooking the lake. Emily was upstairs with Geneva helping Nell get ready. She was stunning in a flowing cream-colored silk gown with elbow-length puffed sleeves, a square neckline and six-foot train. A veil of sheer voile attached to her hair, which was piled high in the back.

When she viewed herself in the full-length mirror, the tension around her eyes disappeared. She looked closely at herself and saw an attractive woman. Then she saw the reflection of Emily standing behind her looking on. Her thoughts drifted as she tried to see the two of them through Charles' eyes. They were almost opposites in physical characteristics. Nell's blond hair was almost white, her skin was ivory, her torso thin and willowy. Emily had a shapely figure, her slim waist exaggerated by her curvy breasts and hips. Her thick curly hair and dark eyes were set in a broad face. Nell was frozen in her own thoughts.

"All set, dear?" her mother interjected, bringing Nell back to the present.

Nell sighed. "Yes, I suppose so."

"You look so lovely, Nell," Emily said and smiled at her in the mirror. "You are the perfect bride."

"Perfect," Nell repeated.

When the violin played the wedding march, Maynard met Nell at the top landing and walked her slowly down the front stairs and into the living room where everyone was crowded in standing. Michael wore a lightweight brown suit over a cream-colored shirt with a matching bow tie. Nell had to concede he made a fine looking groom. The couple said their vows in front of the ornately carved mantle, their reflections showing in the beveled glass mirror. Nell repeated the words from a faraway place, an inner sanctuary of her own making.

When the ceremony ended, they all went outside where tables were laid with roast beef and ham sandwiches, potato and fruit salads, savory cheese muffins, berry pies, and jugs of beer and wine. Hannah and Peter had provided the alcohol and presided over the pouring of it. They were jolly as ever and had clearly started drinking early in the day. A mandolin and banjo player joined the violin player and they provided lively music.

Michael and Nell danced together and then were joined by others. As the evening wore on and the frogs tuned up from along the creek, Nell found herself sitting beside Charles.

"You look so beautiful in your wedding gown, Nell," he declared softly just for her to hear.

She looked closely at him and managed a small smile.

"Can I bring you a drink or some dessert?" he asked.

She continued to gaze at him and her smile faded. He looked at her concerned and narrowed his eyes. He suddenly had an unsettled feeling of menace. He shifted in his chair and then seeing Emily approach, he gestured for her to join them. They sat for a moment and then rose to dance together. Charles hand rested casually on Emily's waist as they made their way to the dancing area. It was at this moment, on this festive day, that Nell reached into her reticule and pulled out the tincture to dose Emily's red wine. Nell's commitment was unwavering. The deep betrayal she felt was palpable even on her wedding day.

Michael drove Nell to their small apartment above the post office where her parents had delivered her belongings earlier that day on their way to the wedding. Others were leaving at the same time and they played at racing and joking back and forth, as they made their way along the dirt road out of the hatchery property. When they arrived at the post office, Michael helped Nell down, kissed her cheek and left her as he unhitched the horse to pasture across the street. When he joined her upstairs, she was already in her nightgown under the covers, looking uncomfortable. He undressed and slid in beside her. He moved close so they were touching head to toe and said softly in her ear, "We don't need to do anything if you aren't ready, love."

"It's okay. We should do this," she said. He kissed her neck and swept her hair away from her face through his fingers. Then he climbed on top of her, lifting her gown. She didn't make a sound, but winced at the ceiling. It was over quickly and they slept snuggled close under the covers.

With their close proximity, Nell was able to see Emily every day. Emily had her second miscarriage two weeks later.

I N THE MONTHS AHEAD, the newlyweds learned that Nell conceived on her wedding night to the delight of Michael who could not wait to have a family. He began making plans for them to move to a larger dwelling, and found a house to rent up the Back Ridge Road, still walking distance to his work at the post office. Nell was due to deliver in March.

Nell had always had concerns about pregnancy. She had a feeling that there was an alien object growing inside her and spent much time contemplating her discomfort at the whole ordeal. Emily was by her side, worrying that her friend would suffer as she had. But when the pregnancy reached full term, they all thought everything would go fine. She started having contractions late one evening and the midwife was called. When her water broke early the next morning it was tainted with blood, which continued to trickle from her womb.

Michael was beside himself. Emily remained with Nell throughout the labor. After forty-eight hours of labor, Nell in her weakened state begged the midwife to remove the child. The midwife had to cut her cervix to get her hands inside around the child's head. When she was finally able to pull her out, the baby girl was blue and could not be resuscitated. Nell died an hour later.

Mother and child were buried on top of the small mountain that overlooked Toddy Pond. Michael had a cement headstone made in town. Charles, Emily, Michael, Maynard, Geneva, Hannah, and Peter were there to lay her to rest.

They stood with the minister and wept together on a cold windy March day.

Emily was unable to ever conceive again, a painful realization for her and Charles. She missed her friend Nell terribly and became a sad introverted woman, spending much of her time out walking alone in the woods. In 1904, at the age of twenty-nine Emily became ill with typhoid and died in the house by the lake. Because the federal government now owned the hatchery land, Charles was not allowed to bury her on the hill above the orchard where her children were interred. He buried her next to her lifelong best friend on the top of the mountain overlooking Toddy Pond.

The Fall of a Sparrow

O NE MORNING, BLACK AND White cat caught a bird and brought it to the door still alive. Anne yelled at the cat and stomped her foot and the cat dropped it and ran off. She picked up the little sparrow and saw that it was still very much alive. She ran out to the chicken house Bret was constructing to get advice.

Bret had been working on this deluxe chicken house for over a month. It was no ordinary structure. It was solidly built of two by fours and stained to withstand the weather. It included a shingled roof, Dutch doors, and ten nest boxes. He had spent so much time making it nice that Sarah joked about installing stained-glass windows in it.

"Daddy, look," Anne demanded holding the little bird in her cupped hands. "The cat had it."

"Is it injured or just frightened?" he asked.

"Don't know. Maybe both," she said worried.

"Make a place for it to rest and see if it recovers," he advised.

Isabelle found a box and they put a towel in the bottom and placed the bird in it to see if it might recover. They got a small dish of water and dipped the bird's beak in it, but it was too frightened to drink. Then they dug up a worm from the garden bed to see if it was hungry. The worm was actually a night crawler and far too big for the tiny bird.

The next morning the little bird was dead. Anne carefully wrapped it in a piece of blue and yellow calico she found in the sewing room and tied it closed with a scrap of ribbon. The bundle was so small and weighed hardly anything. She found a garden hand trowel in the garage and walked up into the woods where the old orchard had been. She found a small clearing in the tangle of underbrush and kneeled down to dig a grave.

The soft, mushy top layer of debris was six inches deep. When she finally found the dirt beneath, it was soft and easy to dig. She went down just a few inches and saw something solid in the dark humus soil. She picked it out and brushed the soil away. It was a flat stone with a metal rim. She scrubbed more of the dirt away and held it up to the light from the sky to see it was purple. The metal part was tarnished a dark color. She slipped the treasure into the pocket of her overalls, placed the bundle in the ground, said a prayer for the little bird's wild soul, and covered it with dirt. Then she spread the leaves back over it so it became invisible, all the while thinking of the babies buried somewhere on that same rise of ground.

When she came back to the house, Isabelle was standing over the box. She was about to ask if the bird flew away, then saw Isabelle's dirty knees and hands.

"Why didn't you wait for me?" Isabelle asked.

Anne shrugged her shoulders. "I don't know. I guess I wanted to have a private ceremony."

Isabelle put her arm around Anne's shoulder and said. "Let's go clean you up." She found some other pants for her and gave her the fingernail brush in the bathroom.

"Where did you bury it?"

"Up in the orchard," Anne said.

"Good. That is the perfect place," Isabelle said.

Before Anne took off her overalls, she reached in the pocket and pulled out the trinket she found. She held it out to Isabelle who put it under the running water to finish cleaning it.

"This is really neat," Isabelle said.

"What if it is the charm that Nell stole from Emily?" Anne asked.

"Wouldn't that be something," Isabelle mused. "Are you going to show Mum?"

"Not yet. I want it to be a secret between us. Okay?" Anne said looking into Isabelle's blue eyes.

"Yeh, it can be our secret," and she handed it back to her little sister.

LYDIA'S ANIMOSITY TOWARD ANNE continued. Though Anne felt like a different person at school, as soon as she was in proximity to her sister, the harassment occurred and made her feel sad and angry. Whether it was on the bus ride home, playing outside, or up in their rooms together, Lydia was always irritated with Anne. She showed intolerance of how she looked, what she said, and how she acted. After a particularly cruel day, Anne would lay in bed at night with her heart pounding feeling the rage and hurt that she suppressed during the day. She knew that if she showed Lydia she was afraid or upset, it would only fuel Lydia's meanness.

Sometimes, when she lay in bed trying to calm her mind and fall asleep, she would wish for justice. She would wish that something bad happened to Lydia to show her that she was not invincible. She would think about them growing up and Lydia having a bad life because of what her mother called karma, a universal force that gave people what they deserved.

That winter, Lydia received ice skates for Christmas. They had been watching the Olympics on TV and Lydia wanted to learn how to dance gracefully across the lake like a ballerina. Isabelle had a hand-me-down pair Sarah had found her somewhere the year before. Anne did not have any skates yet, but she went with her sisters to the lake to slide around in her boots and watch the others practice their skating.

On one of these adventures, Lydia took a bad fall right on her tailbone. She started crying and saying it really hurt. They all went home and Sarah made Lydia a hot bath and gave her some aspirin. Sarah said it was probably just a bad bruise.

In the days and weeks that followed, Lydia did not recover. She complained every day that it really hurt to walk, sit, or lay down. It just really hurt. Finally, Sarah decided she needed to see a doctor. Dr. Teagan in Bucksport ordered

X-rays and they went to Ellsworth for that. The orthopedist called Sarah the next day.

"I am sorry to report that your daughter has ruptured two disks in her back. No wonder she has been in so much pain," he said.

"Oh, no. Poor thing. What do you recommend," Sarah asked.

"First of all, I am ordering some pain medication, Vicodin. But we need to get her scheduled for surgery."

"Surgery?" Sarah thought for a moment. "What is the prognosis? Will the surgery get her back to normal?"

"It should, but the recovery will take time and effort," the doctor said. "She will need to stay home for about three months as sitting will be painful. And she will need to go out and walk many miles a day to make it heal properly."

When Bret came home from work, she told him the doctor's report. He paced the floor, feeling so much compassion for his daughter. "Should we have taken her to the doctor sooner?"

"I don't think it would have changed the result, but it would have gotten her into surgery sooner," Sarah said.

"I feel so sorry for her," he said.

"Me, too. But she will be all right. We will see her through," she said and gave Bret a sad smile.

Then she went upstairs to tell Lydia, as well as the other girls, what was going to happen. Sarah would work with the school to find Lydia a tutor so she would not fall behind in school. The surgery was scheduled for the following week.

That night, Isabelle woke up and heard Anne crying. The door was open between their two rooms as it usually was and Isabelle came and sat on the bed.

"What is the matter?" Isabelle whispered. It was late and everyone was in bed asleep. The house was silent.

"It's my fault. About Lydia," Anne whispered between sniffles.

"What are you talking about? I saw her fall. You were nowhere near her."

"But I got really angry at her. You know how she treats me. And I wished her harm," Anne said.

"So? You can't make things like that happen by wishing them. What are you talking about?" Isabelle said.

"I can make things happen. I have the amulet. Remember, I showed you?" Then Anne told Isabelle about what happened on the playground with everyone ganging up on the mischievous boys.

Isabelle was silent. Then she gave Anne a big strong hug and said, "We need to talk to Mum tomorrow about this."

"Okay," Anne sniffed and pulled the covers up higher around her neck. "I didn't mean to do it," she said and started crying again.

Isabelle laid down next to her whispering comforting reassurances until Anne finally drifted off to sleep.

The next day after school, Anne and Isabelle waited until Lydia was busy reading a book and went to talk to Sarah downstairs. Anne put the amulet in Sarah's hand. She turned it over and over and had Anne tell the story twice about when and how she found it and why she thought it was the amulet from the letters.

Sarah was quiet, thinking. Then she wrapped her arms around Anne and held her tight. "Honey, you cannot blame yourself for Lydia getting hurt. These things happen." She looked into Anne's eyes and saw clearly that her words were not convincing.

"Let me keep this for now," she said wrapping her fingers around the stone. "I will keep it safe and think about what to do."

When Bret came home from work, she said she needed to talk with him in private. Just then, Lydia came in and the conversation turned to how she was feeling and if she had taken her pain medication on time. The medication made her stomach hurt and Sarah asked what she wanted to eat.

It was not until all the girls were in bed that Sarah told Bret the story about Anne and the amulet.

Bret shook his head, sighed loudly, and gave Sarah a sideways look. "Sarah, why have you insisted on nurturing the imaginations of our children in this direction? Ghosts, spirits, magic amulets. What are you thinking?"

Sarah sat still and felt, not guilt, but mild irritation. She wanted her children to explore the unknown. To believe in miracles, to look for mysteries in life. Finally, she said, "Well, nonetheless, I would like your assistance in ceremonially disposing of this object. Whether it is magic or not, Anne needs to be relieved of it and we need to honor the extreme feelings she has over all this. We cannot marginalize her deeply sensitive little self."

He thought for several minutes, then said, "What do you suggest."

"We should take it back to the woods and bury it. This makes me sort of sad, because the truth is that it is a beautiful object. With the silver polished up, it would be worth some money. But, Anne is worth more than any bauble," she said.

"Yes, of course she is. Let's be rid of it," Bret said.

The next Saturday, they all walked up into the woods to the top of the rise above the orchard. Bret dug a hole about two feet deep, just to make sure the alleged object of horror was never found again. Sarah took the amulet from her pocket, gave it one last look, and handed it to Anne.

"We don't know why you came upon this stone, Anne, but it is yours to release back to the earth," Sarah said.

Anne looked at Lydia and said, "I am so sorry that I made you get hurt. I love you and never want to hurt you again," she said with tears in her eyes.

Lydia looked at Sarah and then back at Anne and said, "You didn't do it, I did. I fell on the ice. But I know you think you did it. I forgive you for whatever you think you did."

Anne nodded her head and then held the amulet over the hole and dropped it in. Bret picked up the shovel and filled the hole back in, then they all scattered leaves and pine needles over it until you could not see that anything had happened there, and they all went back down to the house.

Lydia's surgery was a bad chapter in her life. She was in the hospital for a week and then home bound for three full months. The school recommended a tutor who came a few times a week. He sat in a chair near her bed, while she reclined and they discussed her lessons. Interestingly, he had been Stephen King's roommate in college, spurring further discussions about the occult.

Lydia was supposed to walk ten miles a day, which seemed like a ridiculous thing to even attempt in the dead of winter. But she did try to go out each day and walk up the hatchery road, where she encountered foxes, rabbits, deer, and ravens, which were naturally determined to be bad omens. These were dispelled by throwing salt over her shoulder, eating garlic, and other tried-and-true cures for such things.

The Blessing of a Child

I N 1973, ISABELLE WAS fifteen years old and a junior at Bucksport High School, when her life entangled with that of the handsome captain of the football team. Guided by mistaken wisdom that all teenagers possess, they purposely became pregnant to seal their fate together in marital bliss.

Sarah was by then a registered nurse specializing in pregnancy and childbirth. She sat in a chair by the window in Isabelle's room, while Isabelle lay on the bed staring at the ceiling. Both of them tried to decide what to say. Isabelle had broken the news the day before to both her parents. Bret was understanding and supportive of whatever choice Isabelle made. Sarah thought the matter deserved continuous conversation until everyone could come to terms with their emotions surrounding it.

"I definitely did not think you would be the one to provide me with a first grandchild," Sarah said. Isabelle did not reply.

"The one bright spot in this misadventure is that your body is at the perfect age to deliver a baby, despite it being inconsistent with current social norms," Sarah said. Still no reply.

"Has he told his parents yet?" Sarah asked. Isabelle nodded. "And what did they say?" Sarah pried.

"They said that these things happen. Same as what Daddy said," Isabelle answered.

Sarah scoffed. "Well, yes. They certainly do. Always have and always will. I am sure."

"You have to dig deep and decide if you want to raise a baby instead of graduating from high school and then going to college, which was your plan. You could give this child up for adoption to a deserving couple instead," Sarah said.

"No, I am keeping this baby," Isabelle said decidedly.

"You realize that a child is a person that will always be in your life. It doesn't end when they start school, or when they go off on their own and start their own family. It never ends: the responsibility, the need for you as their mother, or the bond that will make you suffer every heartache the child ever has," Sarah said.

"I know," Isabelle said quietly.

"And that is what you want?" Sarah asked again.

"Yes," Isabelle said.

"Would you want me to deliver the baby when the time comes?" Sarah asked.

Isabelle turned and looked at her mother and her eyes welled with tears. "Yes, Mum. I want you right there with me."

"Okay, I will be there. And are you sure you want to marry him, because you don't have to. Women raise children on their own, but it is not easy. Actually, no matter what you choose, there will be nothing easy about your path I am afraid."

"Yes, I want to get married as soon as possible before I start to show," Isabelle said.

"Along the way, I just hope you will never give up on your dreams. Children can mean postponing dreams, but never give up. You are smart, you can still be and do anything you want, it will just have to wait. Will you promise me you will never give up?" Sarah asked.

"Yes, Mum. I promise I will never give up on myself or my dreams," Isabelle said.

"Then I suppose we had better get busy planning a wedding. Given the abysmal financial situation of the couple in question, I suggest we plan to have it here at home, alright?" Isabelle nodded. "Daddy can escort you down the front stairs just like when Nell got married. And you can say your vows in front of the fireplace mantle in the living room."

They sat in thought for a moment.

"Everything will be okay, Mum," Isabelle said.

"No, I am supposed to say that to you. Everything will be okay, Isabelle." And they both smiled at each other.

When Sarah rose and walked to the door, she heard scuffling on the other side and opened it in time to see Anne launch onto her bed.

"I see," Sarah said crossing her arms over her chest. "And I suppose you heard everything?"

Anne's face broke into a big smile. "We are planning a wedding!" She cried, clearly elated.

It made Isabelle laugh and Anne came and gave her a big hug.

The wedding was lovely, attended by the immediate family members on both sides. Isabelle wore a slender silk sheath with a slight trailing train in the back. The wedding snapshots looked like they were taken in the jungle. Bret had become interested in house plants. He obtained cuttings from neighbors and when these were mature, he made more cuttings and kept expanding. At the last count before the wedding there were 110 potted houseplants filling the living room and dining room.

Isabelle and her husband stayed in the guest room until Sarah helped deliver the baby there, a beautiful little girl named Jessica.

THREE YEARS LATER, BRET accepted a management position at the hatchery in Hartsville, Massachusetts. It would be the last move before retirement and would greatly enhance the value of his final pension. Lydia and Anne were upset to leave friends and apprehensive about the move, but mostly they did not want to leave the house that had been home for thirteen years.

Isabelle now lived in Bucksport with her new little family and another baby on the way. After the moving van left, she came alone to give the house a final cleaning and say goodbye to that place that had shaped their lives in so many ways. She was the last one of them to be in the house.

Twenty years later the house was torn down because it was too expensive to heat in the winter and had no air conditioning in the summer. Not that it would matter much since there was no insulation in the walls or attic. The Department of the Interior decided upkeep on the house was a burden. Elements of the elegant architecture went to the local historical society, and salvage companies took the rest.

Anne was in her thirties living in Montana when she heard the house was gone. It gave her nightmares where she wandered the house, seeing it half intact and half destroyed. She wondered that if the house remained, if her spirit might one day haunt it, forever reliving her childhood there. She worried about the spirit of Emily. Would her soul rest now that the house was gone? She hoped that Emily successfully found her way to a new venue, ever warmed with the laughter of children.

Postscript

ONE NIGHT IN 1953, Jenny could not sleep, burdened with fears of a monster under her bed. Sarah found her rolled into a ball, shaking with fear.

"Come on honey, we are going down there to face this together," said Sarah, pulling Jenny out of bed by the hand. Sarah got on the floor and wriggled her way underneath the bed, secretly congratulating herself for having run the dust mop under it the day before. "Well, come on. You have to do this, too," she called up to Jenny who was standing there undecided. Finally, she got down on the floor and wriggled in next to her mother.

"Now, as you can see we are the only ones here," Sarah said.

"But the monster comes out later," Jenny said.

"How much later? And where does it come from?" Sarah asked.

"I don't know," Jenny said.

"Then we will wait," Sarah said.

They laid there and talked about idle things for a while, and then during a pause, Sarah drifted off to sleep. As she began to snore, Jenny considered the discomfort of spending the whole night there. She nudged her mother to wake her.

"Oh, sorry. I guess I drifted off," Sarah said.

"You were snoring," Jenny reported.

"Oh! That is very good. Monsters abhor snoring. I feel sure that monster is packing up and permanently moving elsewhere as we speak," Sarah said.

"You think so?" Jenny asked, in wonder.

"I *know* so!" Sarah said emphatically.

They crawled out from under the bed and Jenny climbed under her covers.

"Better now?" Sarah asked.

"All better," Jenny said. "That monster is packing his bags," she added with absolute conviction.

"Goodnight, sweetheart," Sarah said and kissed Jenny on the forehead.

"Thanks, Mom," Jenny said, followed by a big yawn.

"I am always here for you, little one."

❧

IT WAS SARAH'S FIRM belief that imagination set the stage for creativity. She would no sooner tell her children there were no monsters then tell them to jump off a bridge. Life was full of monsters, both real and imagined. She nurtured her children's minds and souls to make them strong and self-reliant. She believed in them.

Anne and Lydia finally became fast friends when they reached adulthood. Lydia had no recollection of treating Anne badly until they talked about it years later. Lydia supposed she must have come to terms with whatever plagued her about her baby sister when they were young. Anne also learned that all of her sisters had nightmares about their childhood home after hearing it had been torn down. That house during those years shaped their opinions of themselves as much as anything. And it turned out Jenny and Lydia were not the only Vikings. They all grew to be resilient women, though Lydia was irrefutably the most warrior-like.

To be fair to all, Bret and Sarah never helped their children financially through higher education or any of life's inevitable challenges. But when they died, they passed on Bertha's savings. All those years that she was paid in Anheuser Busch Company stock was untouched. Because Olga never had children, Elsie was able to pass it all to her children, and thus eventually her grandchildren. The secret of Halley endured until Anne found a 2010 census record online listing her as the eldest daughter of Bertha, after which she quite literally disappeared. Bret had never heard of her.

Evie's love of cooking led her to open her own successful catering business in Tucson. Jenny became a successful jewelry designer, selling her wares at high-end resort gift shops. Isabelle taught creative writing at Vermont College, helping students find their own inner voice. Lydia moved to the Dominican Republic and ran a beach-side B&B while painting mermaids and tropical fish for the tourist trade. And Anne moved to her grandparent's farm in Oklahoma where their spirits could watch over her.

Acknowledgments

Though this is a work of fiction, it relies heavily on my childhood memories and those of my sisters', who helped me immensely with this manuscript. Thank you Vicki Sims, Judy Schafer, Suzanne Purcell, and Katherine Purcell for always being there for support and good counsel. And thank you to my husband Josh for patiently enduring my obsessive passion of writing.

About Author

Carolyn Purcell Jaco grew up in rural Maine with four sisters. She studied literature at Montana State University and earned an MLS degree from the University of Oklahoma, focusing on history and cultural geography with an award-winning thesis. Through four decades, Carolyn's career in museums included positions at the Museum of the Rockies in Bozeman, Montana, and the Columbia Gorge Discovery Center in The Dalles, Oregon. Now retired in rural Oklahoma, she is a fulltime fiction writer.

Also by this author: *Beneath A Barren Sky*, 2023, Scissortail Press.

Find Carolyn on LinkedIn, Facebook, and at email calyjaco@gmail.com. Please review this title on Amazon.